UNA VITA DI STELLE LIBRARY
A.V. Italia S.r.l. Group
VAT number 03624001206

PUBLISHED AUGUST 14, 2021, BOLOGNA

Tacit assonances

Tacit assonances

This novel is a work of fiction.
Names, characters, places and events are either figments of the author's imagination or used fictitiously.
Any resemblance to real places or events or people who really exist or have existed is unintentional and purely coincidental.

A lifetime of star libraries,
A.V. Italia S.r.l. Group
VAT number 03624001206
August 6, 2021

Tacit assonances

TACIT ASSONANCES

Francesca Terrazzino

Tacit assonances

PREFACE

An incredibly multifaceted and multifaceted author. She writes romances as pulp. She pollutes Lansdale and creates echoes to King and she invents without the modesty of the beardless writer. It will amaze you by freezing your thoughts and you will understand what the fear of your breath is as you read these pages. A concentration of adrenaline, suspense and twists. Real ones, well given, like protagonist's uppercuts. You wish you hadn't read it, because the impalpable doubt that the same events will happen to you, in a banal town, will creep up on you the frighting, sharp, dirty thought of being a speck of nothing against each destiny is raging. This is what happens to the protagonists of Tacit Assonances. Businesswomen become spirits, wrestling champions, young avenging heroines. Nothing, really nothing, is as it appears, everything is discovered and the novel that firstly seemed a hard rose, becomes in a Times New Roman beat, a rhythmic thriller by the burning content.
A small advice, if you're anxious and mildly impressionable, switch to the usual Friends series and forget Tacit Assonance.

Tacit assonances

CHAPTER ONE

"Cut the boring moralizing! I like a man with a big cock! And don't piss me off with your usual Jew-bashing stories...it escapes me why at my age I shouldn't wear skirts or cleavage.

And I don't see why you shouldn't do it: diet, expert hairdresser, manicure and a nice dress and I'm sure you'd close business as easily as I would. Now go, I'll expect you tomorrow with the sales report and I hope it will make sense to you listening at me."

I had raised my voice, these fresh graduates from school and baby bottles wanted me to understand that it was complicated to sell my product, complicated to achieve market prices and to stick to the business plan we had presented in January.

Complicated unless you presented yourself to the clientele in a model outfit, or prostitute, in other words.

I felt neither a model nor a prostitute wearing Valentino's satin jacket-pants suit. The problem was underneath... under the jacket a lovely black La Perla lace negligee and the exuberant whiteness of my breasts, winking at diaphanous hags.

I embarrassed them.

I was too faithful to reality, to the truth.

In my yardstick of values, truth was represented by the gentle scent of wisteria in bloom, reassuring as a timeless tunnel of scent, in which time itself paused, getting lost.

I liked to be provocative and defiant. I knew that my success was due to the beauty and sensuality that men craved to possess. Due to the idea of me, long tanned legs ankles as thin as a London motorway lane to Yorkshire, gently alternating grassy green hills with the ever-present Louboutins as perverse question marks. Do you find me attractive? Do you like me?

Why do you hide behind silly chaste clothes and cover up, when society unmasked our real thought: to possess, to touch, to count the inches of bare skin lying on the beautiful silk bed before intercourse.

Everything ended up there, like a voracious or wanted funnel: advertising, thoughts, fashion, commerce, values.

Having sex.

Make lots of it and good quality.

I had understood this at a young age and made an art out of it.

I sold beauty products.

I was selling them to everyone, through any means possible.

I was not a speaker, I had no talents. I didn't have a college degree and my culture was of average, middle-class, provincial relevance.

Yet I was relevant to this century because I was beautiful.

I always was.

Beautiful and sensual.

And men wanted me.

At their side to brag, in bed to flatter, and in business to use my very weapon.

I think using beauty was really my greatest intelligence.

So maybe I had a talent too.
The talent for non-interpretation. Reality revealed itself to me absolutely in its truest essence.
I read in the men's eyes, my victory and took advantage of it.
Why should I regret it?
I was happy and rich.
And by the time I was forty-five, I could boast a nice capitalized S.P.A..
I traded in body products, make-up, hair, sold all over the world and maybe I should have thought listing on the stock exchange and to open a holding company.
She was the majority partner and the founder. Every decision needed my approval.
To get to my office on the Champs Elysees in Paris I had excited and seduced, conspired and manipulated like the best, Brutus, Cassius, Judas.
Just the right people.
The ones who made me powerful to thank me.
I was Italian. I arrived in Paris to advertise the usual over-the-counter perfume, I was immediately noticed for my amber complexion, raven hair and eyes.
Certainly hair, eyes and breasts were not a rarity in the fashion world.
But the eyes were different.
You would dive into a liquid of sea and sky and land burned and salted, poor and dirty.

Then you will emerge from poverty in the still waters of revenge and ardor, of dreams and hopes. You will emerge in the fire and grit born of poverty and desolation.

Daughter of the repetition of the same smells, the same tastes that wipe out ideas, zeroes opportunities.

Yet her chance was there. In the blue of her eyes. In the black of her hair. In the scent of skin tanned and salted by sweat and the scorching heat of his Italy.

And from that vague citrus smell that greeted you in the stony fields.

From the love that always brought me to my land.

My name is Anna. I liked to pronounce it always in Italian, dragging the consonants to lengthen the palindrome name, truncating it immediately as on a sheer cliff in the bizarre waters of the Apulian coast. Anna and away we go, a pirouette dive from a medium height hill, the stones between our toes flying in the air thrown by the impetus of the flight while we take the jump, arms and legs curled up. The world turned around and turned around again, sky and sea, sea and sky and then Anna cuts through the salty, foamy, fresh and welcoming water and takes it all in and then returns it with a long breath of refreshing and beneficial air.

Anna, as the villagers say it, in a loud voice, calling the beautiful woman and inviting her to turn on the narrow streets, walking on the cobblestones of the village with her skirts fluttering and her tanned legs, smooth and inviting.

I was left alone in the meeting room, I stared out the window, it was raining outside. The weather in Paris was not mild.

They knocked.

“Come on in, I'm ready for round two.”

"Anna, we need to broach the subject of the sale of the majority shares of the Cosmic Corporation to Art Defender S.P.A.. It's a lucrative deal, I want to outline the benefits to you, you have the meeting with Art's CEO on Thursday in London. You need to prepare."

Art Defender, I'd forgotten, I had to make a decision. The one who spoke softly was my accountant, the master accountant, the one who held all my bank accounts even offshore, the person I trusted the most. A bald, bespectacled little man like any transparent accountant in the common imagination, present, with an elephantine memory, as witty and patient as he was stocky and of precarious gait.

He felt stable before only his counts and their realization.

I looked at him, blushing, like a demure teenager.

Did he dream about me? Did he imagine me?

English by birth, French by profession and mine for everything else.

"Leonard... yes, come on, let me see." with him I used to speak in English, an English known for the marked Italian accent, but which the English themselves liked because it had the taste of the exotic.

He shakily approached me with his laptop in his hands, like a whimpering infant.

He laboriously attached the pc to the lime and started the slide show.

I wasn't interested. I wanted a man. A hot man specifically, hot like an Italian.

"As you can see we would be returning a significant sum, we are talking about 10 million euros, with an initial exposure of 500 thousand euros and the achievement in 6 months."

"We give them 51% of my first company, we bill a lot in cosmetics, this year we increased 3% with no added costs." I replied.

"You're not convinced." It was evidently a statement of fact.

No, I wasn't convinced, creating my first company had cost me to prostitute myself profusely to one of the richest backers of the Cosmetic Corporation, to get the interest-free money, the money that had allowed me to get started.

He'd wanted to humiliate me and tie me up and beat me with some kind of whip across my bare skin. And smiling, I had to swallow his juices and his disgusting seed.

Yes. It bothered me quite a bit.

He had an unpleasant habit of squeezing my right breast. I touched it now, to make sure it remained like a fearless little soldier in place. Darling, you did your job stoically. The pervert had eventually shelled out five million non-interest-bearing, purely on merit of donation to the person of myself.

Never returned.

No signed paper.

Giving up now 51% of what I consider the best deal I could have ever conceived of while alive and awake, I was annoyed.

Of course they were only paying me for half the shares twice as much as it took me to create it.

Afterwards the poor man had come to beg my love... love!?

Did he really think I enjoyed hanging like a salami from the canopy of his bed in Switzerland?

And did he ever have imagined that my enjoyments were artifacts, for he was a man thought to himself and stuffed with his ego.

How many years had it been? Four, maybe almost five years.

"Anna, with that money we can upgrade the other derivatives and grow them."

"Leonard, you know I am not an educated woman, but I have learned that whoever comes first gets all the benefits from the market. The other companies even if we invest will always remain less fruitful because they came later. Imagine Coke, it's not that Pepsi is less good. It just came in second."

"Anna, what are you saying, the time in the graphs is clear, look, within 2 years if you boost logistics and online advertising, you get to the same results as the first Corporate even with sisters."

"No. We'll give them 49%. For a lower cost, of course. Tell the CEO I'll go in and arrange the transfer myself. But the signing authority will remain with me."

"They might not take it. And look around for companies that are coming into the same market overbearingly equal to us."

"They'll take it." She would have moved on to injecting herself with a few cc's of Botox.

She touched her lips. Good. They were always full, but she could do a glycolic acid cleanse and a draining massage.
"I know what you're thinking. I've known you for many years. And you're beautiful, always." She paled again and paused a little, demurely.
"But you might not get the consent of the Art Council."
"Why is that? Do I look a little old?"
"No exactly, you're beautiful." He swallowed.
"Come on don't make a big deal out of it, what is it?" I was surprised.
"The CEO is a methodical, morose and uncompromising Englishman. Known for his moralism."
"So? What's the big deal? Is he a gay?"
Honestly, he had learned that even gays could appreciate watching ... There were no constraints on sexuality when combined with the ability to perceive the other.
Everyone wants to.
You should understand what art was.
"No no. I don't think so at least, of him I have no news to that effect. He is only a real Englishman, of the Lutheran school."
"What do you mean? Don't English people fuck?" I purposely chose to be vulgar, I was enjoying noticing his embarrassment.
"Anna! What are you talking about? Of course he has affairs of bed. But not both business and bed. Besides, he's an English nobleman, a duke, connected to the lineage of Queen Elizabeth's cousins. I know it

doesn't mean much to you, but English people are very attached to the crown and their displays of honor."

"I don't follow you, it's not like I want to turn England into a Republic, let the islanders believe and vote what they like! I just want to give up 49% and not 51% of my company. If the Lord cooperates fine, otherwise a kick in the arse!"

"You get inflamed right away... it's your peculiarity." He sighed. He used to love me. He was forgiving me.

"You know I'm superstitious. Selling 51% is the same as selling the company, and it's the first one we've formed. I wouldn't want it to be bad luck. This one, this Lord, he'll get over it."

"I believe England is not ready for your landing."

We looked into each other's eyes and burst out laughing together.

"Book me a flight. I want to arrive a day early and have a casual date with this little man. "But first, the coiffeur and a full day of beautifying myself... massages, etc, contact my surgeon."

"But you don't need anything...you're just beautiful."

"I need, I need... like all beautiful women to gratify my reflection."

He nodded and walked away sadly.

He knew I'd fuck the CEO and maybe the entire board of Art Defender Spa.

"I didn't quite understand... "I had just landed in my usual suite in the city at Piccadilly Circus.

"Mr. Hoffman had a pleasant message arrived for you which we left in your suite. He saw to it that you were notified immediately." The concierge was extremely diligent.

"Perfect let me be escorted to my room. I wish to rest, do not pass calls." My heels ached, the plane had brought 40 minutes late, the limo driver had gotten lost and didn't recognize me, and it was still raining. I longed for the warm sun on my skin. Even the September sun, the one that doesn't burn you, but only warms you benevolently by penetrating your flesh and invigorating your bones.

I could feel the dampness on me. The leaden, cold marble of loneliness.

"Alfred will show you to your rooms. Enjoy your stay, Miss Sevaldoni."

He opened the doors to her suite, always beautiful, on the top floor, furnished in beige, soft in the carpets, comfortable in the armchairs, spacious and cool in the bed.

In the center of the room a beautiful little glass table entirely covered with a huge bouquet of virginal white roses.

I approached. A gift, of course.

Mr. Hoffman's, evidently.

Men give to possess.

Women accept, pretending not to notice.

She opened the elaborate matte card with baroque squiggles at the corners.

Bad taste, too much effort.

"I must decline our early appointment. Instead, I await you at the day set by the Council with your best intentions for us. M.H."

He stood me up.

He was evidently terrified that I would make him deviate from his purpose.

I picked up my phone, quickly scrolled through my schedule, in London, Peter was licking pussy like few others. It was fine, to take the hassle out of those fake flowers.

CHAPTER TWO

The water invigorated my numb muscles, cool, invigorating, flowing fluidly with cheerful mumbles on my skin.

With Peter I had enjoyed myself intensely, the orgasm was still inside me.

Gently.

He had taken me with commitment and passion, lest I forget my devoted pleasure, languid Peter, blond hair and with almost transparent skin, but two very clear blue eyes that seemed to be looking at a faded watercolour.

And with such fervor towards him, such incurable comforting submission I stared at the crumpled sheets of the large double bed.

I was rather sorry to lie still where I had consummated my orgasms.

The moods clashed with my desire for cleanliness and order.

It was like running away and coming back. But with the castle in order.

I picked up the phone and asked for a car and for my room to be made up.

“What displacement Miss?”

“A comfortable displacement.”

“Do you want the driver?”

“No.”

“Fifteen minutes Miss and a comfortable Smart car with an automatic transmission and right-hand drive would be ready for you.

I'll charge it directly to your room.”

"Obviously."

I wore white satin underwear, a pink turtleneck sweater and skinny jeans. Crocodile knee-high boots so there would be no mistaking the nature of the huntress.

It was raining.

The Smart car waiting for me was neon pink, lovely, I complimented the concierge, He had played me without hesitation.

I blushed. You liked me, didn't you?

How wonderful to feel like a magnet of sensual desire.

I entered the cabin, the car smelled of rubber and plastic, vaguely of orange car freshener, overall extremely pleasant.

Always the scent of new cars was pleasant to me, nice as a new love.

I set Brighton on the navigator, it was distant, true, but the longest wooden bridge in the harbour had always been one of his favourite destinations. The little bars laden with sweets and games, with flavours and novelties, novelty as an opportunity to hit the little bear and take home a kiss. The kiss of the beautiful one on duty, of the greediest girl, of the friend you dream of at night.

And walking even in the rain-laden wind on the aged wharf was pleasant and familiar because of the brackish air that wounded his nostrils, cold and salty as winter in his land.

I could benefit from a long, lonely weekend, the orgasm I had just achieved would last for me at least two days before I felt the familiar languor mount.

I wanted a change, Peter was already boring me.

I should be ready for the Art Defender's Council the following Monday.

I turned off my phone.

Quiet.

Loneliness.

I pushed the accelerator.

I wished I could find everything in a man, maybe it wasn't possible anymore.

Perhaps it was probable to find something in every man and be content with the puzzle, make it pleasant and comfortable and move on.

Right-hand drive was really tricky, maybe it would have been better to slow down.

But the light drizzle annoyed me.

I felt invincible.

Nice and overpowering.

And the crocodile boots, the roaring rock music, counterbalanced with the sound of pistons and connecting rods pumping power to the engine.

It was impossible to slow down the race of his life.

Egocentric, absolute or dissolute mistress of a small cosmetic empire.

I caressed one breast, it was swollen and turgid with excitement, rolled down the windows and the sharp air lashed my face, moving the black strands of my hair madly.

Drops of moisture invaded the cockpit.

The windshield wipers began to move swiftly, it was raining.

I would have slowed down at the next corner.

Always at the next hurdle.

Suddenly I saw popping up on the road what could probably look like a cow.

A stupid cow. A useless, herbivorous cow that would soon end up with a trivial side dish.

I wanted to avoid it, thinking of the mess that would result on my glamour car, a mess of flesh and blood and guts.

Avoiding it, I lost control of the car, the dampness of the road, the tires, perhaps underinflated or underperforming, the Smart car skidded to the left and ended up on the grass for a long stretch, fortunately the road was flat, until it came up against some boulders. Stuck like a sword in a stone.

The airbag exploded, the belt trimmed my torso and shoulder and held me to the driver's seat.

The smoke enveloped her.

Good deeds don't pay off in the end.

New bodywork on that box of a car, would have cost the same as a new car, hopefully the engine wasn't compromised, otherwise it was toast.

The insurance company would have enjoyed taking it off your credit card.

Well, Saint Mercedes who could build cars, she didn't have a scratch on her.

I hoped the cow would be hit by another driver, a British one, so I wouldn't have any problems with the local police.

I tried to unbuckle my seat belt but it was stuck, perhaps a safety feature in case of an accident.

This was a problem, tight in the belt and compressed by the air bag it was obviously tricky to call for help.

But I needed help, evidently.

I said what in my memory resembled a prayer.

I almost had to laugh, at the thought of my omnipotence being vilified by a mere cow.

It would have been more honorable to denounce a herd of buffalo, or horses, wild horses.

Or bulls. Here, bulls.

From a distance my ear alerted me the sound of another engine nearby, a different engine, rounder and crackling, loud and galloping. Not muffled like that of a car. Perhaps a tractor, though it had its own snappy speed, far from the clarity of a tractor.

The noise grew louder and louder, and then it suddenly stopped.

She couldn't see anything, the smoke and the air bag blocked her view.

The door opened suddenly, all of it, entirely, and with the impetus. So much so that he imagined it fell to the ground under the strain it had taken. The light and the cold air entered the cabin.

The smoke escaped.

An escorted silhouette with other senses not eyes bent over me.

"Are you okay?" he asked in a perfect English accent, Oxford maybe or Cambridge or some college renowned for polo, cadet uniforms and the chance to feel important.

"Yes, thank you, schiacciata... "I mumbled in my very Italian English, learned at night classes and applied with constancy in every meeting so much so that it became a third language, a hybrid of the two, exotic, as many said, but which suited me.
And then when did they ever really listen? When he showed up at meetings with clear ideas and the guepierre glimpsed under his skirts? Or rather when she decided not to wear underwear and let her alter egos learn that without a shadow of a doubt.
"I'll help you. Be patient, I'll get you out. I'll be right back."
"And where do you want me to go?"
I had to laugh. But II realized right there how easy it was being a hero, me squeezed like a sausage between the seat and the steering wheel.
He was a fast hero.
When I returned to my visual quadrant, there was something strange on my head. A motorcycle helmet and two large goggles with orange lenses. A black scarf with small uniform prints was lowered his chin, revealing a hint of a brown, soft beard.
I thought he really wanted to play hero, now I understood the particular noise, he was a biker.
Perhaps I could momentarily aggravate my condition in favor of his gesture.
He had stopped, wanting to make himself useful. And he had a square jaw, quite sensual. Lips hidden by a moustache. Very white teeth.
"Help me, please...I can't breathe." but I shouldn't have to exaggerate, otherwise I would end up in the hospital instead of his arms.

"Yes, forgive me for being too slow, I don't want to hurt you."

Hurt me?

I noticed the long knife in his hands.

Just like that, the seat belt was cut.

He popped the air bag. With a long hiss, it deflated in front of my face.

My locks got all tangled. He burst out laughing.

It sounded like a long fart. Certainly not befitting a first amorous encounter with a stranger.

"If he laughs, it's obviously not that bad."

He looked annoyed. He was right, the testosterone god needed to be satisfied, he was the man.

Me woman.

"I don't feel well, no. Can you help me out, I'm afraid I'm going to faint."

"I don't think you're going to faint."

"Oh, yes I swear to you, I'm dizzy and have the beginnings of nausea. Please support me."

He held out his arms for me to lean on.

I looked like one of those little Lego men you put on and take off little cars.

He wore a distressed leather jacket with the Triumph logo written in black on the chest. He had broad shoulders, the big chest of a sportsman. Or otherwise the jacket's armour plating exaggerated the proportions.

He was wearing a pair of jeans, old or specially faded. And dark leather biker boots.

I noticed he hadn't even removed his gloves, black leather.

It was very tall, very large, taking up most of the sun's place.

And below him, the half-light seemed almost blissful.

I let him take me, he lifted me out of the cockpit in a few flying moments.

And I flew right up like a Lego soldier, diligent.

My nipples hardened.

They were my faithful radar. I was looking at an interesting man, as long as he was really still hidden from me by his helmet and big biker glasses.

"Let's move away, just in case there's no engine leakage."

"Yes."

He supported me from the side and literally carried me two meters away, next to his bike. I think one step of mine was matched by three of his.

"Sit on the bike, it's got a kickstand, it's safe."

I looked at the bike. Round headlight, slim tank of shiny black paint, steel chrome, lozenge-worked leather seat, also black.

He was smoking out of the low-rise exhaust.

"It scares me."

He laughed, a long, guttural, hoarse smacking sound.

"Don't be a child, it doesn't do anything to you. Just don't lean on the mufflers, because they're red-hot."

I was silent. Motionless.

I felt like a child.

I was out of my country, even my adopted country. Alone, without my purse, credit cards or cell phone.

I wished I could have a husband to call upon. A thoughtful husband who would impersonate a husband and come to my rescue on the damp moor.

A husband who was a little piece of that puzzle that when put together would perhaps have given me happiness.

Happiness. For that stranger, probably, happiness was there in front of me, two wheels and a handlebar, and the chrome gleaming in the sun, as soon as it had deigned to pop up in that cold country.

"All right. I'm gonna sit on my butt, not sit." And so I did.

"Are you dizzy?"

I shook my head, no.

In fact, I wanted to fuck him, but it was indelicate to confess it.

"Maybe you can at least take off his glasses."

So we can see what you look like.

"I don't find it necessary, not least because I intend to retrieve her belongings and take her to the nearest town. Police and hospital."

"How are you going to get me there?" but he was already far toward the car.

He took my purse, a black Chanel shoulder bag, and the suede jacket I had abandoned on the passenger seat.

He came back towards me, his legs were so long. He crossed with long, sure strides our distance.

"Wear your bag. Over the shoulder. I'll give you a helmet."

"How?" I didn't understand.

He took a helmet from the leather bag anchored to the left side of the Triumph and handed it to me.

A small black leather bowl, with rope safety lacing.

"What should I do with it?"

"Wear it!"

"Wear it?" I sounded stupid. I didn't understand, did he want to take me on the bike?

I had just had an accident!

"Yes it is a regulation helmet, and by law you are required to wear it fastened if you get on a motorcycle, for your safety." he sounded falsely patient.

You don't fool me, you're not patient.

"Come on, it's getting dark soon. And it's dropping temperatures, it's certainly not equipped with the proper attire." he left in suspense, as most women do.

Of course he'd already x-rayed me, I was a woman, I'd ended up with my little neon pink car seat like a gemstone against boulders and now of course I was throwing a tantrum wearing a bowl, on my hair fresh from the hairdresser.

"Yes, I'll wear it. And I'll ride with you. But I would have preferred that with your cell phone, you called an ambulance and a tow truck."

"The nearest town has only one ambulance, and necessarily I think it properly should be reserved for more serious cases than this."

"Ah... thank you."

"As for the tow truck, I don't think it's convenient for you. It's a long way from town. I'll get my mechanic to come down here with the tools and the winch, he'll get it back up and running again. In London, because that's where you're from, of course, he'll get it fixed."

"Okay." I was stunned. Maybe I'd even widened my mouth in an O of amazement and ecstasy.

I put on my helmet, the brunette hair couldn't fit so I let it loose.

"You'll be cold, keep as close to me as you can, I'll shelter you from the air. Put your shoes on the pedals, not on the mufflers. OK? Do you understand? I'm asking because I understand you don't speak English well."

I nodded, I understood, I understood.

I straddled behind him.

And I held on.

He started the engine, the roar thrusting mightily into my ears.

CHAPTER THREE

I closed my eyes, the cold air lashing the skin of my face, like little icy whips.

I had once happened to whip an old Greek shipowner with a velvet cat-o'-nine-tails.

The filthy man knelt, letting his elderly, drooping intimates dangle, waiting for me to wound them of the humiliation of the bland rod.

And he enjoyed the penetration of an adult game that I strapped on with a belt around my waist, with the tulle mask over my face, with the mask so I wouldn't remember the thrill and illusion of power, that moment gave me and that were instead just humiliation and shame when I woke up in the morning.

But a lot of money had been given to me by that conduct. And I took it all.

And I forgot.

I hid a little behind the massive, muscular shoulders, hoping they would conceal the cold, inappropriate feeling of no longer being a virgin, a virgin of emotion.

The curves and the body that with the bike in unison went down to the right and up again, and then down again to the left and up again, hypnotized me. I just wanted to get lost.

And if I had let myself fall, than I would have abandoned myself in the vacuum of air.

Not asphalt under the circulating wheels but air and water and dense limbo to erase, purify, sanitize leading me back alive and pure to a new me.

Maybe I let go of the grip from his waist because the big hands took my runaway wrist and put me back where they belonged.

Like a diligent Lego construction.

Volatile and fearless, he himself had created the scenario in which rescued and saved me, than lead me to the Hospital.

I caught sight of the lights of a citadel with the slits in my eyes. The fog had descended, the darkness hiding us from view, the headlights barely illuminating banks of dense, smoky fog like in children's nightmares with wolves and evil ogres.

The engine lost a few revs, we were slowing down.

I could hear him screaming something inherent in the fact of our supposed arrival, the tiredness was so much now. Made of hours and days and years of loneliness.

He stopped.

"We have arrived. It's the hospital in Brungenwald. They will cure you."

I got tighter.

He turned, forcing me to loosen my grip on his chest.

"Get off."

I looked at him astonished.

"You may not abandon me here."

"No."

"Please. I'm cold. I'm scared. I'm not used to it."
What falsehood, I was used to being scared and cold and the sort of emotional barbarism that had allowed me to win all the time. But not now. I really needed to lean in.
"I have an important engagement, I'm already late, I really need to let you go in alone, then I'll come back and see you and inquire about your health."
"Please, I feel like crying, you certainly don't know but I really need you to stay with me. I can't do it alone going in there, calling the tow truck, fixing the car. Please."
"How are you feeling?"
"Stunned."
"Yes but really how do you feel?"
"Good." I was ashamed.
"Then I'll take you to my house. You'll sleep in the guest room. Mrs. Boff will take care of you. And we'll arrange everything from the chalet. That way I can get to my appointment almost on time."
"At your house?" Images of naked bodies made their way through the mind clouded by the English moors, and rumbles of vintage engines, and little badges on biker scarves and orange goggles that concealed discerning, serious eyes.
"Either at my house or here. But choose quickly because I'm in a hurry."

"At your house." and a shy smile escaped me that a virgin wouldn't really have widened, perhaps more that of a hungry tiger spotting its prey in the foliage.

"You seem satisfied."

"Yes. I am." Why lie?

He started the engine again.

We moved away from the town but only for a short time, the bike wedged in a narrow path, the drizzle was falling insistently. I was now completely wet.

I imagined a hot shower, steaming tea and a lit fireplace crackling briskly for me.

But I was getting colder and colder. My hands were numb and icy, even as I tried to protect them in the folds of my leather jacket.

Finally the bike lost revs and seemed to stop.

I could see silence at last. And a house shrouded in the red foliage of a vine perhaps, I could not see well.

It was an old heath house, with a sloping red roof and walls covered with ivy and climbing roses and wide rectangular windows in the vast rooms over which towered stone and stone fireplaces and extraordinarily wide flues.

"Get off."

A small red gravel, ran down the path end to the steps of the front door.

The door opened slowly and a slice of light like a slice of cake opened up to illuminate us, two dark silhouettes in the evening darkness.

"It's raining, sir, you'll get wet. Come on in."

Probably the maid.

I hadn't come down yet.

"Come, Madam will give you some hot soup and dry clothes."

He took my hand.

I didn't know what to make of myself, the shy or the bold one I was.

The virgin or the prostitute.

The white or the black soul who had known so much and so many ways of pleasure.

I was wobbling. And I felt dizzy inside both of them.

Maybe I was the chrysalis and could still undergo a metamorphosis to please this kind man.

Maybe I could still be better and forget.

I was nameless to him.

With him, I couldn't remember my name.

Descended.

I shook his hand.

"What a warm welcome, and you can smell your broth. We'll have a cup right away. Thank you."

"Sir Beaumont has been waiting for you in the study for about 30 minutes. Perhaps he likes you in the study?"

"No, for the young lady. I will hurry with Mr. Beaumont and be with you. Please look after the Girl, hot bath, dry and comfortable clothes, and especially her broth."

I watched the scene as if numb.

I saw him take off his helmet and release a thick reddish hair, small curls cut short to be tamed probably.

Very clear aquamarine eyes. And freckles on his aquiline nose. If he hadn't been wearing a beard, he'd have looked like a teenager on a motorcycle.

Yet the white in small hairs on his reddish-blond beard and temples and eyebrows and a few small wrinkles at the corners of his eyes and lips said he was not beardless.

But nice.

He stared at me.

The helmet was swallowing me up and detracting from my beauty.

The cold had whitened the flesh of his face and lips. His eyes were wide and astonished by the day. By the new day with its wagonload of new emotions.

"Go."

He turned and walked away.

CHAPTER FOUR

The boiling water ran over my flushed skin.

Steam clouded the glass shower stall, and timid drops of damp water vapor dripped from the red stone checkerboard that completed the austere English shower.

A waterfall of gushing water and from the walls jets of steam from mignon taps, hidden and chromatically multicoloured.

I felt like being reborn, enveloped in the rain of water, the rhythmic tapping evacuating my mind of thoughts, adding the emotions of peace and protection.

I would come out of the water, wrapped in a warm, soft, white, clean terrycloth.

I would wear new clothes and impersonate a new me.

A simple, meek woman.

Helpful and humble.

Casta.

No past.

It would have allowed the illusion to replace the heavy reality.

And light would experience.

I looked at the creams and balms at my disposal, they were carefully selected and branded.

Women's choice, of course. Brands like Chanel, and Prada. Yves Saint Laurent and an excellent Estè Lauder cream, in golden micro-

containers of biodegradable rubber, all laid out and neatly stored in the toilet.
Complete absence of dust on the crystal that protected an antique marble with veining in various shades of gray.
An elegant little chair with a seat of burgundy velvet, and arched legs of gilded wood small inlaid acanthus leaves, completed the elegant female toilet. The thick woolen carpets welcomed my bare and still damp feet with soft steps, leaving small footprints as light as shadows on the white wool, as on the white snow just laid down.
From the stained-glass window, in great rectangles, the rain beats on the panes, like the rain on the glass of the shower just left. The same sound of heels on wood, of small hammers on nails, like insistent ideas. The ones that lead you to change.
The beauty of the room had led me to an almost obsequious veneration and she hesitated to touch, preferring to skim. The large bed in the center of the room was a wrought iron canopy with no voile concealing but with a very soft white mink fur resting softly as a blanket.
A fireplace of red stone and large river stone occupied the entire wall in front of the window. It was lit. The wood crackled joyously. The smell of oak and birch and burning pine resin was imbued with the warmth of home. The glass vaguely tarnished.
I approached the bed. Luxury no longer frightened me. Now I could own it and use it without any fear. But this was luxury and culture, grace and charm. It was the luxury of a family that had always lived

in ease and culture. Objects were chosen for their significance and matched old and new with swaggering class.

A drop of water disfigured the composition of the bed, between the soft, white pillows and white sheets and the white, cream-colored fur of the mink in their winter clothing.

A drop of water, fallen from me.

And already disfiguring. Like a little devil in the paradise of shapes and uniformity of colors.

How was he to appear tonight before this proud and aging family?

I felt chameleon-like and eager to curry favor with these gentlemen.

The favors of that gentleman.

I imagined that her beauty would not affect him. He was surrounded by beauty.

I would have to study its gaits to capture its essence and use it to my advantage.

I imagined that sex couldn't interest him.

The coat of arms stamped on a fireplace stone crackling with winged griffins meeting, crossing tails and forked tongues in winged intercourse on chequered reds and whites, told me of honor and morality. Of ethics and virtue. The virtue that had made him stop on the side of the road and not allow me to wander alone through the hospital in the desolate town.

I hadn't been able to notice the wedding ring; the gloves had concealed the nakedness of his hands.

But a woman had been there, healing, creating, nurturing.

I decided not to wear make-up. I dried my hair, which smelled sweet around my pale face.

They had left me a comfortable beige cashmere sweater and a pair of women's flannel trousers, also beige. Comfortable raw wool underwear with small lace inlays completed their suggestion.

Comfortable fur slippers, slightly oversized warmed my little feet.

I decided to appear shy and awkward.

I decided to believe that I was shy and awkward.

It was my art, to understand what my antagonist desired and to satisfy that desire. For that they had paid me, lots and lots of money.

To satisfy their desires I had transformed myself many times. And I had learned more and more. Games, contrivances, seductions, some even amusing and always to my advantage.

And it was always worth it, why it always became beneficial as it materialized.

Here the reason was still lacking, perhaps the path was the reason.

This man was a discovery, his morality a challenge.

I lightly caressed the mound of Venus covered by the heavy flannel of the donated trousers. A gentle caress, loving and grateful for my feminine features.

I opened the door, I was ready.

Soft notes took over the hallway of the wide staircase.

Piano, I supposed.

They became more and more intrusive, until they filled the entire room.

I followed them.

Now red-hot embers fed a central stove in the middle of the room, suspended from the ground and conical in shape. Semi-circular glass windows surrounded it as if in a shining embrace. Soft lights formed small yellowish rays under the fabric lamp shades, cleverly arranged to follow the moonlight peeping through the glass.

A record player amplified by multiple hidden speakers, diffused notes of a piano, along with the dirtiness of the record and the old, aging audio.

Two armchairs of antiqued leather, perhaps a black-white spotted cow, sat in front of the stove, warming themselves. On one of them, the owner of the house was listening to music. I could see the back of his head and the thick red hair and a wrist and a fist on which he rested his cheek, leaning three quarters of the way to the armrest of the rough chair. Perhaps he was resting.

Or he was waiting for me.

It was vaguely embarrassing, I did not wish to disturb the moment of quiet absorbed in the intent of listening but I did not wish to be excluded from it either.

"It's Debussy."

I transfixed, as if I had been discovered with a huge sack of gold nuggets, lowering myself through the striking windows among the roses in the garden.

"How?"

"Come sit and listen with me."

"Here I am."

"Do you like it?"
Of course the question didn't ventilate any other answer, that yes, of course I love it.
"I love it, it's so evocative."
"Debussy, Clair de Lune."
The record was melodiously harmonizing the keys with small high notes, in one hand, and in the other a cascading vault of fast bass, like a balance calming the sounds by dispensing rhythmic and melodious beauty, straight to the heart through the ear.
I couldn't bring myself to be caught, I remained vigilant watching the rude, aquiline profile, the red beard moustache as it bound from nostrils to lip, escaping in length to the sides of the mouth and in thickness, while in the middle in the dimple, it remained shorter.
In the light of the burning embers, they looked even redder, and the small white hairs masked themselves in them, almost disappearing.
The eyes with thick, very light lashes and small reddish blonde arches for eyebrows.
His high forehead, slightly wrinkled, with small horizontal marks running through it like parallels in the globe, lit even now as he listened somberly to the music.
Lively instead the beard, thick, red, as if to presage that the shady thoughts could be mitigated by a more serene verbal vision, and that there was still much to think but even more to live, especially on his motorcycle, in an era of young boyhood always alive.

A thick, wool-colored, cream, turtleneck sweater struggled with the mesh and small unruly hairs escaped to hide in his neck.
I wished I could pull down the neck of the silky sweater and smell the man's scent.
A fire seized me. A sudden flush of heat flooded me, mocking me, reminding me that I was still me, a liar, devoid of culture, art, a social climber who had climbed over the naked bodies of my competitors, denouncing, photographing, debasing and stealing.
I made myself tiny in the spotted armchair, hard and uncomfortably firm on the oak parquet floor.
The record ended, rasped on the platter and croaked hexamely.
"Did you like it?" He stood up.
He was mighty in truth. Like all Englishmen of Anglo-Saxon birth and derivation, he had broad shoulders and a pronounced torso typical of the race, like the Scots accustomed to the temperatures of the moors, the cold winds, and the desolations of the rocky plain.
He removed the record. He stopped the record player. And turned around.
Slowly and thoughtfully to get it right, and in the process of thinking the action, a thought to the conversation and how to formulate it. And I, reflected that these three actions, took longer than expected to think about how to respond to any benevolent conversation.
And how in truth he didn't mean anything other than, let's get rid of the clothes or I'll get rid of the clothes.
I stared at him high and peremptory.

"Yeah, sure. I don't know about that."

"You don't like classical music?"

"In truth, I never listened to it."

"Where do you come from, you have a very thick accent."

"Italy. Apulia."

"Interesting. Hence the raven hair and olive complexion. But the eyes are not of your land, so clear, of the turquoise of the stony-bottomed sea as I have only seen it abroad."

"Italy suffered several invasions, especially in the south. Germans, French, the races also mixed during World War II because of the rapes and raids by both the Nazis and the partisans."

"True. Were you born in a small town? Like most stereotypes about her countrymen."

"Yes. Unfortunately at the little village by the sea. Just that sea you mentioned, with the turquoise water, such as I don't think I've seen many times, the bottom of rocks and crystal clear water, and the real fish, not the reef ones of course, but colorful ones, swimming ashore among the rocks and seaweed. Still a beautiful place."

"You seem to miss it."

I felt like looking at my hands. Long perfect pale pink nails, fingers with few but valuable rings. Once they were just girls' hands.

"Yes. Another way of life. Genuine and ignorant. It was simply truth. I reflected that the glitz of money confuses reality and suggests interpretations, illusions. “

"I'd like you to listen to Caruso."

"Caruso?"

"Yes in Hauser's interpretation for violin."

"I don't think I've ever heard it."

He turned, searching from the bookshelf behind him, for a record, yellowed in its cardboard sleeve, as vaguely creased as the best dress ever.

The symphony of the violin reached me quickly, warm, sweet, poignant.

I felt wrapped up like in a soft cloth blanket, like in the sincere embrace of a lover in love.

He reached over and took my small hand, lifting me from the chair.

He hugged me. Not tightly, but gently. And swinging, he taught me to dance with him.

I rested my hands on his shoulders, far above me, and my cheek to his chest.

The aroma of cologne and clean wool and wood in the stove reached my nostrils. I could hear his pulse with mine in my ears and in my ears again, the music gently lulling us both.

The record ended, the turntable stopped. It crackled in stereo.

"I guess you're hungry."

I nodded. I was devastated.

The emotion of the feeling had seized me, and he was as sweet and affectionate as I could remember. Like my mother who loved me and would have wished for me anything but to become a prostitute in a mask.

"The Lady of the house, my maid, as you may have guessed, has left us a superb dinner."

"Fabulous."

"Follow me, I'll lead the way. You'll need dinner and a good night's sleep, and in the morning I'll have you driven to London, to your hotel, where you'll handle the Smart car pickup."

"I would like to stay a few days here with you." Of course it hadn't been clever, confessing it so openly but the load of the day was getting to him.

He looked at me surprised.

"Why?"

There, a man who didn't play games, who didn't hide and was real.

So he didn't need the words.

It required considerable effort, answering the truth.

"Because I like you and I've never met anyone like you."

"I have many faults."

"I'm sure more than you."

"But I'd rather have them seen right away."

"I don't want my parents to ever see each other," and it was true. I would have died if he had learned my life.

"Let's have dinner first. You must like cooking."

I kept looking at him fixedly. He had incredibly clear, limpid blue eyes, and perhaps I could have read his thoughts through, as in a Rembrandt panel, read the emotions of the young woman sitting on the bench.

He left me appalled, seeming unperturbed and ironclad towards my own.

He stroked my cheek with a rough fingertip.

I opened my lips instinctively.

I wanted to.

"Let's go Italian girl."

And he took me by the hand. And again I seemed to dive into my past, as from the stones of my land, into the water that washed away the impurities of salt and sun and sand.

CHAPTER FIVE

The man was muffled, as if his self-expression was in space, around him.

A few words, calm and direct in meaning, and then around him, in his element, a whole range of sounds that represented him, as if he had a score of notes in space that left the banality of noise to embrace the complexity of melody.

Like a string quartet that fearlessly followed and anticipated him, and in time represented the moods and mysteries.

We left the room and its lonely crackling, the record player stopped, outside far away the tapping of the rain on the fine glass of the old windows.

Dragging his rough woolen slippers across the old wood floor, he led me to the dining room. An apotheosis of scents and bright colors, muted by the light of two long scented candles that, lit, faintly illuminated the laid table. Other candles of stubby size and colorful colors burned in glass vases like water glasses, and occupied the entire kitchen in alternating spaces.

The tapping of the rain was always with us, familiar. The table in fact was positioned in front of a huge glass door which presumably in the light would show a garden of roses and willows in front of the back of the Saxon country house.

The rain was no longer falling on the glass but on the pavement near the opening, presumably a pergola was protecting the entrance.

It beat incessantly on the cobblestones of the doorway, highlighted as an orange pen stroke by the sliver of light coming in from the kitchen, like spectrums of rain.

The environment though dense with smells was cooler.

A kitchen with large aluminum burners, like the kitchens of gourmet restaurants, occupied an entire wall alone, topped by a shiny aluminum hood, wide and low to capture the entire smoke coming from the fires below.

An antique porcelain tureen with little flying cherubs towered limply on the free shelf. A capacious ladle was immersed in it. A small, loquacious rivulet of spice-scented smoke rose from its half-closed lid.

He led me by the hand to the chair in front of the stained glass window, the place was richly set.

Plain and flat plates with the familiar flying putti, and gilded edges on the plain plates that looked a warm salmon color in the candlelight.

Two glasses, one for wine and the other for larger water, both crystal, light with small aerial decorations, white, on the rim and on the more solid base.

Silver cutlery, larger than normal, ancient evidently, with handcrafted features and with a coat of arms engraved on their end. Again the griffins knotted in an amplitude of forms, circling roughly in the small space of the spoons and forks.

St. Gallen lace napkins, white, ethereal, like the tablecloth.

"I hope you like capon broth, hot, with homemade croutons."

The croutons were resting in another small porcelain container, all unequal and toasted with oil. The smell of the warm, fragrant bread was delicious.

"Yeah, everything looks great."

The absence of his words, had drained them from me as well.

"Be my guest. I'll serve you, if it's all right. I let the servants go home."

"Yes." And timidly he observed my hands gathered in my lap.

I didn't recognize myself. I looked like another me, like a mocking doppelganger and showing me a life, a chance, not my own.

"It's very hot." He was almost whispering, the rain overpowering every sound, even that of thoughts. The candles winced irreverently, showing the shadows of gasps, the veils in the astonished eyes.

I followed with my eyes the ladle dipping and reappearing laden with broth, to spill slowly into his deep dish. The thick, thick smoke rose quickly along with the lighter, more subdued smell of spices and meat.

"Please taste."

I took the heavy spoon, slightly larger than normal, like the old spoons, those of my great-grandparents when I could remember me as a child on a hard wooden table and bowls of hot soup.

The hubbub of relatives, the stroking of hair.

With that load of love I had grown up with, how could I have transformed myself to such an extent, distorting myself?

Hunger. He still remembered when the first compromise. In front of a jewel. It was so incredibly bright, it seemed to be fed with its own energy as if every atom of the sun had gathered within it, to nourish it. And to feed the vagueness that one jewel could effect change.

Yet that jewel had changed, the accepted jewel had been succeeded by flattery, compromise, lies and tricks. When I subjugated my first partner for the shares of the first company, threatening to extort much more with photos and videos that clearly compromised his social status, I was now a thief and a liar.

He voluptuously inhaled the warm smell.

Images of bodies entwined stood before me.

How can you erase the memory?

And still at the crossroads of a new choice, will it be enough to choose with virtue?

How many virtuous choices will be necessary, like a reverse Monopoly, you become poorer but more virtuous, you will no longer have Victory Course but the medal of the good explorer.

"I imagined you to be a chatty woman. Instead I hear you quiet and meek. Perhaps you don’t know the English language well. Should I speak more softly or articulately to help you?"

I watched him. He wished me to be meek. And quiet.

I imagined undressing him slowly, in the dim light of the fireplace, my breathing punctuated by the drumming of the rain.

I smiled, lowered my eyes.

It was already mine.

That's why I was rich and powerful. Because I was the predator who waited in the unconscious corner and grabbed the desire, transforming it into reality. And I made myself irreplaceable and a master of that reality.

"Perhaps it's shyness, yours?" He insisted, his spoon insistently left on the plate, soaking in the broth, waiting for me.

I decided to lift my eyes, low on makeup but deeply blue.

I knew that my eyes were beautiful. They were beautiful because clear eyes make us imagine a good Goddess, a nymph, a gentle youth, they were beautiful because the blue was intense and the iris bright with the health of the body. Because they were deep and even without makeup the thick black eyelashes of my barren land, were the gift of many dinners with little food, of a poor land but with a raw and strong beauty that never in the contrast of colors, you could see in other races.

The thick eyebrows always black, on skin made pale by leaden England.

I looked at him.

I noticed a slight redness in his cheeks.

I imagined that he hadn't had a woman for a long time, and that he wasn't practical at casual conquests, or that it wasn't easy for him to take advantage of the opportunity.

He was hesitant. He wanted to show off his culture, but he could tell I wouldn't be impressed. He couldn't figure out how to catch me.

And I wasn't going to let him understand. I liked playing at being better, different, as pure as he imagined, fearful and virginal.

He shut up.

He sank into my gaze.

I saw him lost thoughtfully, thoughtful of bodies clutching, and nails clutching sweaty backs.

He had big hands, long fingers, with bitten nails and short on purpose.

I wasn't wearing any rings.

Pale hands, with a few blond hairs escaping from the bony wrist.

I imagined them grabbing and squeezing my slim waist to push themselves in.

"I worked in England for many years. I understand the language." I moved my lips slowly, knew I had a full, voluptuous mouth.

He placed his gaze straight at my lips that moved slowly to cadence the words, slow showed the tongue between my teeth to form the words.

I slipped my tongue over my upper lip and mechanically moistened first one lip then the other, leaving my mouth slightly open.

My blush increased dramatically. I abandoned his gaze.

One me, inside, was smiling.

I wanted a man who would win me over, actually. It was always so simple.

"I'm very tired."

"I'll show you to your room."

He stood up, his body was mighty, in the small English kitchen. The rain was beating the roofs.

"Come."

He took me by the hand and got me out of the chair.

The broth overflowed from the plate, the glasses clinked.

Were they waving at us?

The chair squealed.

Close to his chest, I was coming in just above his shoulders, feeling tiny.

He had a mighty chest, you could see it through the rough wool sweater. Strong pecs, the result of exercise, sweat on the equipment and the effort and vigor of pushing his muscles.

To my nostrils came his scent, an opiate scent of man. How I would imagine cowboys riding ragtags to round up the herds, or rally racers as they took on mountain curves to be flattered by the passionate audience.

Are you married?"

"No."

He arched his right eyebrow. He doubted.

I showed him my hands. They were free of rings. No marks left by the sun.

He took them both between his hands. He enclosed them all and brought them to his mouth.

H laid a shy kiss on my little fingers all curled up inside his strong, enveloping ones.

I felt my sex getting wet and opening to receive a caress from those lips as well.

"Come on. I'll show you to your room."

He held up a hand and with a quick twirl guided me towards the stairs.

I could smile now, I was behind his back, unseen.

I was looking forward to a night of fire.
The man was obviously used to cold, bony, pale-skinned women.
I would have drowned him in the sea of my land, in the mood of my greedy sex.
I imagined he was an inhibited amateur. It would have been a fun game, melting the barriers, letting the overpowering arousal spill out as I would have wished in a tall man with those broad shoulders I was observing now before me.
He came to the door of my room. He stopped, turned around.
I read the doubt, reached for the handle.
I squeezed his hand. It was encouragement.
"Has anyone ever told you that a God should be more decisive?"
He smiled.
"I guess you don't really know what you said."
"I know better. Come in with me."
And I let go of his hand, sliding down to the crotch of his pants.
I found his sex. I found it aroused and stunned. An unsuspected hardness.
He took my wrist.
"Are we there yet?"
"More like a beginning than a point."
"Poor me who gives that I have seen you, I have wished nothing but to fall into a bed with you."

"Then open the door and take off my clothes," I whispered, I too was aroused and yearning for his lips. I knew he wouldn't give them to me right away. But I wanted them.

I closed my eyes. I focused on my desire.

I imagined his body undressing for me, vigorously mounting me, holding my head to penetrate me deeply.

He slipped into my lace panties, a trickle of warm humor. I was ready.

"It could be a mistake, without knowing each other."

"If I were an angel and could predict the future, I would have chosen this moment with you."

"You look like an angel, a beautiful black angel."

He brought his hands to my hair.

"Then what is Hell? Maybe it would be not going into that room with me.

I prefer to think of you as a beautiful angel given to me for some merit I can't remember."

He took my whole head with his big hands, pulling it back a little with all my hair enclosed in his hands. I kept stroking his sex, feeling it grow as my breath. I unzipped his pants, leaning down to kiss me.

Warm lips came to rest, buttons spread, and made me slip my hand over the flesh.

He took my whole mouth. His tongue all the way inside me. And my head still in his hands.

I slammed into the doorframe and was deliberately crushed.

I wanted to be naked.

I felt my strength pass to him through saliva and tongue rudely invading me.
He left me with a pop as if he had sucked in the moods, the uncertainties, the souls that lingered tightly inside me.
Again.
I ran my hands to his buttocks, stripping them, his pants pulled down irretrievably, freeing him.
It would have been vaguely ridiculous if excitement hadn't prevailed, watching him erect and male and incredibly endowed.
I watched him. He looked at me, red in the face.
I lowered the handle. And I pulled him in by his swollen member.
She took off my sweater and lace camisole.
And he grabbed a soft breast.
He looked like a hungry man; I seemed to perceive now the meaning of lust. But the mind was obnubilated and in clouds of thick steam wandered over his muscular body.
A few long, red hairs escaped the hollow of my armpits, I threw my face and nose all over to catch every scent, and the whiff of a distant male sweat threw me into oblivion. Thoughts and consciousness fled together, leaving nothing behind.
His chest was almost smooth, his skin was soft and toned, his muscles were firm and darting as he rubbed them against my bare nipples.
I couldn't hold out any longer.

I bent down on my knees. And I took his swollen, engorged member completely in my mouth. His surprise was so great that he seemed to want to withdraw.

Then I frantically pushed it all down my throat.

My ears heard a distant grunt like an animal that awakened wanted meat.

He grabbed my head and the whole mass of hair and pushed his whole member down my throat. A gag came from my stomach but I held it back. He held my head tight and I was almost against the wall, impossible to retreat. I had gone from being a hunter to a hunted. I couldn't think, my thoughts were overlapping and accelerated as the strokes of his hips in my mouth, deep to penetrate all of me. Another gag caught me, I tried to expel it but he pushed himself in further. Saliva dripped down my arm, to my elbow.

He pushed again and again and hugely invaded my throat with his overflowing humor.

I could feel it going up my nostrils and out.

Violently I would have to swallow gags and humours and the drops of saliva dripping from my arm convinced me to enjoy and nullify myself in my orgasm.

I let go of his member and hung onto his waist.

I vaguely felt his hand abandon itself in a gentle caress on my hair.

Was this how jockeys petted their horses at the end of the race?

Shame seized me, still mocking saliva dripped from my elbow.

This game was lost. He played me truthfully. No way to lie.

Tacit assonances

The terms of the game were totally out of balance, I would have to come up with something.
Now I was on my knees.

CHAPTER SIX

I had taken a lukewarm shower, now I was wrapped in the soft blankets, an impalpable but warm and enveloping duvet covered me entirely up to above my chin.

I needed a good night's sleep, too much excitement, too many adventures in one day. Too much even for me.

I closed my eyes, the dimness of the room was atonal, a reassuring night colour.

I could hear his footsteps in the hallway, he was busy, back to back to back, maybe it wasn't him, but the maid. For him to stop though, it was beginning to bother her.

I inhaled the scents of the room, lavender, rose, the blankets smelled clean, like cloths just taken out of the dryer, soft, fresh, smelling good.

Still back and forth, sound of footsteps, like they didn't want me to sleep.

I tried to turn on my side, the pillow wrapped around me.

I imagined his sex penetrating me violently, overpoweringly.

The door swung open.

I shuddered in the blankets, and blinked. The darkness was thick.

I recognized the silhouette of a man.

"Ah it's you! You scared me!!!"

The silhouette straddled my bed. He wore sneakers and smelled of musky aftershave. A sub-brand for sure, given the intensity in my nostrils.

I tried to get up. Impossible, with the weight of the man on my torso, my arms immobile under the covers, I could only move my head.
"You scare me! Stop it!"
I heard a soft laugh.
My blood froze. Fear rose like an acidic gag in my throat.
I saw that the man had his face covered by women's tights, his features flattened by the weave of the impalpable fabric.
"Is this a bed game?" I yelled, if it was a bed game, I wasn't liking it.
I tried to kick by forcing my legs together and raising my torso. I was pinned to the bed.
The man showed me a long table knife, the kind used to slice bread, with a long jagged knurling. Perhaps a thin wooden handle in his hands.
My heart hammered in my temples, life had been too short, I wanted more and more.
I kicked and kicked. I saw the blade on me, held in two hands.
I started screaming really loud. Loud? Nothing came out, nothing. A stupid game of fate, even though I had always the word, I died just like that, without being able to pronounce on it.
The blade sank slowly into my skin, a gush of warm blood hit my eyes, blinding me for a second before the pain came, fear had provided the perfect painkiller. It was true that one died before it happened. The terror of death was so vivid and intense that it flooded my body with adrenaline.
I blinked and a stream of blood came out of her mouth, like a rude burp filled with thick, red liquid.

I seemed to utter a vague no, no I don't want to die now. No, when I'm a rich businesswoman and I can fuck whoever I want and whenever I want.

No, thanks. I don't like this movie, let's move on, let's go to the nightlife, let's enjoy youth, beauty and some very alcoholic drinks.

The blade penetrated again, it was set like a beautiful diamond in his sternum.

Feeling my pulse galloping fiercely, I tried again to move my legs. Urine soaked her nightgown. I was dying without panties in my piss. Was I?

Still he heard the blood pouring out, felt it sharply as it leaked out like a broken and collapsed dam. Help.

"Aaa it to" I warble as if at solfeggio to learn languages well.

He stared at the head wrapped in the woman's stocking.

Why?

What had he done?

Erroneously at this moment when I was dying in my own blood and urine, I couldn't think of who was killing me and why. All I could think of was that I was dying barbarically, filthily, that my dead body would be white and hard, with a horrible gash in my chest where once my swollen breasts towered. Now they would be soaked, floppy and hollow, completely uncoordinated in the lintel of her new dead body. Now that horrible cut would continue to widen in me, touching the bones of my sternum and splitting them, reaching the muscle of my heart that pumped and pumped spasmodically the last amplexus. And

slowly penetrated it slumbered in the last lap of blood, the last lap of death, Anna, in the roller coaster, one more, before your flesh cools.
All the humours came out, the bowels evacuated without restraint. The air became saturated, sweat, blood, feces.
His eyes dulled, the man shaded in the darkness, the curtain fell with him.
The scene is over, the show can't go on, the main character is leaving, close the curtain, quick.
And this is how I see myself now, lying on my back on the bed, wrapped in the filthy blanket of my humours. Stinking, deathly white, disreputable. Dead with a man mounting me without really doing it, still straddling me and my shroud pressing with the pressure of his body a bread-cutting knife, with a wooden handle, perhaps.
The rest was darkness and night.

CHAPTER SEVEN

Clara was late, she was always late, because she was lost in thought. Thinking about life, about love, about when she would meet him, where and what expression would he have, of surprise? Of enchantment? Of brooding foreboding?
And what would she look like? How would she have been dressed, styled, made up? Or plain as usual, in her naïve, romanticized twenty-two years of pink.
Clara was still an adolescent with an adult body, long legs, narrow waist, ample breasts and very long straw-blond hair of rare brilliance. It was thanks to her grandmother who always brushed her hair cupidly at dusk before tucking her into her woollen blankets. She brushed it and fed it with honey and lemon compresses to lighten it naturally and she never cut it, so much so that the ends that touched her waist had become almost white.
She wore pretty little flowered dresses, cinched at the waist by rope and fabric belts, and white tennis shoes with white socks tucked in from the ankle to show their lace-embroidered trim.
A lovely, romantic young woman steeped in happy ending romances who constantly imagined that her Blue Prince would arrive, even on horseback, to pick her up and take her to his Palace.
The eyes were vague, a cerulean summer sky blue, and as intangible as clouds in the same sky, lost in fantasizing about her serene princess futures. Blue and large, and they would have made them a true beauty

if only they had rested on people less vacantly. The only real dirt were the intense black eyebrows that enhanced the arch of her eyebrows impertinent and false, sordid and deep, concealing that perhaps in the thoughts of her dreamed by her eyes, the handsome prince would lead her to a bed to finally savor her protected virginity.

She had to get on the bus to the City, her college friends were waiting for her, to celebrate exams passed with good grades and some holiday love to dust off and laugh about.

The libido of her companions was wild and overbearing, the tales indecent to say the least. But they were a laughing matter, for the unfortunate ones always remained alone, and the occasional boyfriends, fled as soon as they could.

She wouldn't run away, because she had learned at the first wail not to let him taste her sex before he was in love with her.

And she had kept herself for it, and still no one had had the honor of slipping a hand under her skirts.

She made the last stretch of the run, her skirt fluttering vexatiously between her knees.

The red bus was stopped at the end of the line, the stationary conductor stationed integer beside the entrance.

In Brungenwald she would have taken a connecting flight to London.

"Here's the ticket!" with one last twirl of her flowery skirt, she displayed the ticket for obliteration, her tapered finger nails bitten like anxious teenagers.

"Get in, please." Atono.

Clara climbed the three steps of the bus and chose a middle seat, free, from the window, the grey seats inviting a light apathy. Light raindrops bathed the glass of the bus, fell drumming, streaking it like tears.
Clara, rummaging through her pink Eastpack, brought out a small black book and a small charcoal pencil. She loved to draw faces of girls, with full lips and winking eyes, even nudes contorting their bodies in sighing amplexes. They were private drawings, of which she felt a conscious shame that had led her to choose a secluded spot on the bus to devote herself to that liberating passion. There she could be the sensual Clara, the perhaps perverse and lecherous one who dreamed of a prince-lover.
The bus closed its doors, we were off.
Well, a sense of relief came over her, she would soon be in the company of her friends in London, listening to them and laughing light-heartedly at their gluttony.
She drew a young woman with long hair, naked with swollen and turgid breasts that fell over her belly and nipples with huge aureoles. A youthful face, posed for a forced kiss, with lips swollen from kisses that promised orgasms, perhaps a prostitute, perhaps a young drifter.
She signed her charcoal drawing in the left-hand corner with the initials C and F, just in time. The end of the line had come. It was time to get off. The connection would arrive in a few hours' time, at 20.20. In two hours she would be in her hostel in London.
"Please disembark. The bus to London has been delayed slightly. You may wait in the passenger area."

The passenger area was a cramped cage with six green plastic chairs. White walls tiled with blue subway tiles. Instinct pushed her away.

It was raining lightly and almost dark.

A light mist was coming in from the moors.

The lights of a yellow sign, Bistrot George, caught her attention, exactly across the street.

She ran across the paved road, covering her head with her backpack, zipping her denim jacket with her hand. The air was cold and uninviting. The door was open. A sound accompanied her entrance, like in the bistros of a few years earlier. Long tables, accompanied by left and right two-seater benches of a placid plasticky, padded blue, cheerfully set up the place. Good, she liked it. The menu offered sandwiches and hot dogs, beer and sodas, and of course some excellent buttered potatoes.

"Good evening," she turned to the lady at the counter, "I'll have a veggie sandwich and a long coffee with a dollop of cream."

"We'll bring it to you, take a seat miss, where are you headed?"

"In London, waiting for my connecting flight."

"You'll have to wait, there's construction going on along the road to London, the buses don't leave at night."

Laconic.

"That's too bad. My friends were waiting for me."

"How can I? I don't know where to sleep. They didn't warn me."

Despondency seized her, helpless little dreamy Clara.

"You can try if they still have any vacancies at the Inn, but I doubt it, surely the other adventurers who were travelling on the bus with you will have headed there as well."
"Oh God, where do I spend the night!?"
"I wouldn't know Miss, we don't have any rooms here. And I'm closing soon, you're the last one I serve. Sit down and I'll bring you your sandwich, then you'll see what to do, search with Booking, sometimes they get lucky and there are vacancies in some House nearby."
She was right, food first, then she would think better of it. She felt too fragile now, the new fuel would be good for her soul.
The plate arrived filled with the fragrant smell of homemade food. The smell of real bread, baked and then toasted, with finely chopped vegetables roasted on the grill, eggplant, peppers and tomatoes in thin slices, and a very soft and stringy mozzarella cheese, melted between the breadcrumbs. It was nothing short of exquisite, the first bite filled her senses with satisfaction and complacency for how good it was, like the first sip of coffee, hot, black, bitter at first sip but with a slight aftertaste of acid from the two drops of cream mixed in.
Sublime, a true treat for the hungry.
Outside came the darkness. Here now everything was in a new mood, she would look for a room that would accommodate her, a House run by some old English bigot who tended budgies in iron greenhouses in gardens of blooming roses.
She would have been lucky this time, too.

She warned her friends, a terse message so they wouldn't worry, the bus had been delayed, she'd catch the next morning's connection. Don't worry, they would still have all night the next day to hang out and chat. She looked toward the glass window, the darkness and fine rain glimpsed in the light of a few nearby streetlights.

The sound of the door made her turn.

In walked the most handsome man she had ever seen. Red in hair, curly, with a red beard covering his jaw, eyes as intense blue as she could suppose the Caribbean sea to be, which she had never seen.

He was tall and probably muscular, broad shoulders covered by a leather jacket, perhaps a motorcycle jacket, with the words Triumph printed on the sleeve at the level of the biceps and a red checkered scarf rolled up around his neck.

Her heart took a dive and then in a drift began to beat furiously. Her cheeks turning purple, she hastily wiped her mouth with her hands, not wanting him to see her with bread crumbs or sauce on her face. But clean, the way she always felt. Clean and honest. Modest and humble.

He looked at her. He saw her. He gave her a barely sketched nod of greeting with his head, to the side, a fraction of a second only, in which he lowered his head and raised it again. A second to realize he was noticing her.

What did he see? A young woman sitting composedly at an empty table with the remains of an impromptu dinner? Accompanied by a backpack and some dreams?

He smiled with his whole mouth, opening the door to perfect white teeth, the result of years of braces, which he was now thankful existed.
She felt obviously dizzy.
The lady from the bistro arrived at the counter and greeted him.
He heard her say, "Doctor Henry, the usual?"
He was the town doctor. A distinguished professional.
Perhaps she could ask for information on where to stay overnight, better from him who was respected and known, than from others.
She stood up.
She took a deep breath.
She wasn't in the habit of talking to strangers.
She approached the counter silently with her backpack in her hands like a small protective barrier.
The scent of man reached her nostrils. Like a mixture of cigar and gasoline, of masculine cologne and saltiness. She felt a slight dizziness.
"Sorry to bother you..." came a faint voice from her.
"Yes tell me Miss." His instead was deep and baritone.
"The bus to London doesn't come until the morning."
"I don't know, I don't know about public transportation schedules."
"No no...I wanted to ask you something else. I'm sorry I didn't make myself clear."
He set two searching, intelligent, discerning eyes on her. She felt her soul uncovered.
"Tell me then? How can I help you?"

He leaned over, was he sniffing her? And what was he sniffing? Fear, interest, that subtle emotion that foretells the intensity of discovery? Was this what it felt like when love became apparent? That trepidatious torment, that perturbing anticipation?

"I well, I don't know where to go."

Better start with the facts.

"Do you require overnight shelter?"

"That's it, a safe house."

"I can telephone the boarding house nearby, if you wish, and accompany you."

Retirement, old people, getting away from him. No that was definitely not what she was thinking about.

"Yes, thank you. I don't have much money on me. I hope it's cheap."

"I have no idea. I don't need it." Dry.

He picked up the phone, quickly dialed a number.

"Miss Boff? Yes, do you have a free room ready? Yes, all right, we're coming. Warm up the capon broth, your specialty. I think the person needs your attention."

Then to her.

"Yeah okay. I have a place for you. Do you trust me?" and he smiled at her. A very white row of regular teeth. A red beard in which I glimpsed silvery threads, two well-trimmed moustaches, always red. And eyes, sincere, friendly, understanding, blue as the sky.

"Yes." It was the only plausible and true answer.

She would have gone with that man anywhere.

"Come on, I'll take you. I'll pay for this. Don't worry, tomorrow you will be in London with all your money and this little incident, it will be forgotten."
"Thank you." She was even moved, my voice trembling slightly. Could it be that a humble and beautiful God was so helpful to her?
It was what she had always dreamed of, a more mature man, a chance meeting, fate blatantly working for her, weaving the web of her happiness. Love that was overbearing and sudden and longed only for its fulfillment.
"We'll walk. It's close."
He took her by the elbow, brushing it lightly, removed her backpack from her trembling little hands and pushed her toward the exit like a puppet master, the puppet.
The street was dark and deserted. The cold caught her, she shivered.
"Are you cold? Do you want my jacket?"
"No no don't bother."
"But it's shaking, here take it, wear it, it's leather, it'll keep you warm."
Smells like cigars and leather and fuel.
"Thank you." Fleeting.
They walked in silence side by side. In front of them stood out in the thick evening fog, an old house in perfect English style, with climbing roses in the porch and small steps leading to an inlaid wooden door. A coat of arms of the family, a lion clinging to a snake on yellow-red colors was set at the entrance.
He played.

Not a sound was heard.

Yet the doorway opened in the fog, letting an almost blinding slice of light escape into the evening darkness. The slice widened, Clara squinted and adjusted her eyes. A smell of leavened bread, vaguely sour, came over her. The smell of leavened bread and wood burning in a fireplace. Good wood, pine or chestnut, the resin it produces was unmistakable.

A chubby, reedy old lady became apparent in the light and smells.

"Sir, here you are. Come in, you have no jacket, you'll catch cold."

"Thank you Miss Boff you are always thoughtful, and your cooking is truly unsurpassed. What have you prepared for us?"

"Shepherd's pie, capon broth and fragrant bland bread croutons and lastly, the tart made with her raspberries."

"Great, meet the young lady. Miss? I realized I don't know her name."

They both looked at her. She felt at school, was it her fault?

"Clara. Clara Freedworth. From Southampton."

"Well well Miss Clara, what brings you out here to the moors?"

"They're waiting for me in London, at college. My friends. I passed my exams with flying colors."

"A student. In what?"

"Architecture and Design."

"Great, an artist. Hence the bitten nails and slightly blackened thumb. Charcoal or pencil?"

"Oh but how do I do it? Charcoal. But they're private, I don’t show them."

"Yes of course. I wouldn't want anything you didn't want first."

The blood rose to her cheeks. What could she ask for first?

"But this isn't a boarding house. Is it?"

"Yes, darling, for heaven's sake, of course not. This is Count Henry's home. The spring house."

"I'm at his house." I looked at him. He probably loved me too.

"Yes, I have no addresses of guesthouses, least of all cheap ones. But the mansion is equipped with many guest rooms, absolutely independent, some heated by imposing fireplaces. It is evening now, but in the morning if you wish before you leave, I would show you the garden and the surroundings, they are disarmingly beautiful. Truly English." He was already calling her by her first name, so maybe he didn't want her to leave, he still wanted time for them.

She was flattered.

"Sure, I'd like that. So we'll have dinner together? And now will you show me to my room?"

"Yes good girl, that is reasonable. Mrs. Boff will show you the lavender room, I think it is the nicest, for a pretty young lady like you. You can rest and get ready for dinner. You will find every comfort."

"Thanks, I can only say that, I guess."

He caressed her with his gaze, running all over her.

He followed the weighted silhouette of the maid.

They climbed the stairs and he opened the door to a huge, lavender-colored room with an imposing four-poster bed on which towered white cream pillows.

It was impressive, to say the least. An English window in small rectangles dominated an entire wall. Outside, perhaps willows swayed in the wind.

"Is it to your taste Clara?"

"Yes, yes, of course. She's wonderful, thank you very much. You're very kind."

"Little duty. Now rest, the Count will be waiting for you at nine o'clock in the dining-room."

And politely he brought the door behind him.

CHAPTER EIGHT

Clara was stunned, but excited.

She had fallen in love with a count, and was perhaps loved back with the same intensity. He had as if kidnapped her to reality and led her to his palace. There he would surely declare his love for her before he left again, and he was as noble as the Blue Prince she awaited.

There he was. He had finally arrived. She was glad to be a virgin. He certainly would have appreciated it.

He set his backpack down on the white bed.

A good smell of flowers reached her nostrils. Underneath another smell, a woman's perfume, maybe Chanel. She didn't know any better. Surely it had been some lover's room. But it was her. The room was for her.

He laid his jacket carefully on the armchair with large red rose prints and the skirt on the wooden feet. He laid it down carefully, laying it down and stroking it.

Then he took off his white tennis.

Those were supermarket shoes. Maybe she should be wearing pumps right now. Like the ladies.

She unbuckled the cloth belt of her dress. And the zipper on the side.

Then he pulled it awkwardly from around his neck.

She wore only a tank top and white cotton briefs. The small breasts were mellowed by girlish nipples. Like the champagne glass her grandmother used to say. She longed for a hot bath. She was alone.

She could indulge on her body. Although a tinge of shame was always lurking. Her grandmother always scolded her that good girls don't mirror themselves naked. Now though, she was going to have a lover, maybe. He would certainly want to kiss her, so it was necessary to aim. She took off her tank top and panties, quickly. She was naked. An instinct led her to the large glass window. It seemed cold outside. Perhaps being mirrored in the window rather than the mirror was less untoward.

She arrived in front of the window. Her long legs, narrow waist, small breasts covered by her long hair. And the blond hair that hid her sex. She touched it in reflection. Then she looked up, the willows swaying furiously. Thunder ripped through the air. The reflection doubled. Behind her was a dark-haired woman with no arms or legs. With a gash in her chest and large misshapen breasts. Her tear-filled, blue eyes were barred. As was her mouth in an unexpressed scream.

She screamed loudly. The scream came out of her and echoed around the room.

The door swung open almost at once. The count and the maid came running in. Clara was still screaming, petrified. She had not noticed her nakedness.

His arms shook her. They wrapped around her, turning her to the window, pulling her against his chest.

"What's the matter?" cried Mrs. Boff.

"Nothing nothing, leave us. I'll calm her down. She's a child. She's probably frightened by a reflection on the moor. I'll take care of it. Please go."

The maid withdrew.

Clara kept sobbing. She curled up all in his body.

"I saw a woman. She was terrible. A dark-haired woman. Oh, God, she didn't have any arms or legs. She was in the window behind me. Oh, my God. It scared the hell out of me. I'm sorry."

"Come on, I'll cover you. It's nothing, maybe a reflection in the woods, a lot of emotions. If you want, I'll give you a sedative. You'll feel better."

"It was terrible, I'm terrified. I don't want to move. I'm scared."

He held her tighter, savored the soft skin under his fingertips. His waist back, he began to caress her slowly, lightly.

He pushed her blond hair away from her neck, gathering it like a tail at the back of her neck. He released and uncovered her girlish breasts. How firm and fresh they were. He wiped the tears from her face.

"Come on little one, it's nothing, you're all worked up. All sweaty."

He whispered in her ear. He was tall even without shoes, reaching her mouth. He laid small kisses on her forehead, trailed his fingers down to her neck, her shoulders and captured a small breast. It filled his whole hand. He continued to kiss her face, her eyes, her cheeks, her nose. With his other hand he grabbed her hair and pulled it lightly down, her face stretched out to him and her mouth opened. She was docile, still sobbing with her eyes closed. The hand on her breast massaged it softly, his thumb and forefinger captured the nipple, it was small and turgid.

He kissed her lips lightly, she opened her mouth and allowed the gap. She looked inexperienced. Her sex exploded and swelled rapidly. He wished he could wait but it was impossible, he had to possess her now. He slipped his tongue in and with his other hand sought the opening of the unexplored sex. Nothing was more bewitching than virgin exploration.

Knowing that she was perhaps the first of a young, immature body and that only he could make her mature to the pleasure of orgasm.

It was hairy.

She stopped sobbing. A small choked sound of pleasure came from her throat. You lecherous little nymphomaniac. She liked it then. Maybe she had staged that pantomime to be found naked. Imaginative little witch.

He picked her up and she spread her legs and wrapped them around his waist in a little gymnastic leap. She was soaking wet. He held her up by her buttocks she harped on his neck. Now she kissed him entirely with her whole tongue inside his mouth. She was inexperienced, greedy, a glutton for flavor.

He threw her down on the bed, all open, naked, her wet sex already wanting.

She didn't cover herself. Turns out she wasn't as modest as she appeared.

She actually looked like the usual cow.

With her arms outstretched above her head, her hair spread across the pillows, her stiff breasts erect.
He opened his pants, He had to get out. He pulled down his panties, He was dripping.
He was going to explode shortly. He aimed the big stiff cock at her naked entrance. Her lips opened for him, he pinned and pushed. What a tight cunt, it made him enjoy even breathing.
Suddenly the whole room fell in unison. A deafening roar, broken glass everywhere. She jumped in bed. He lost his erection. The fireplace lit. It lit itself.
The flame burst into flame. Anna was there. Anna was at the window. Anna, what were you doing at the window?
The girl below him followed his gaze. Her eyes and mouth opened wide, she could see it too. She was about to scream.
He slapped her really hard. He didn't want Mrs. Boff to see her like this with his pants down.
She roused herself, curled up in the corner of the bed.
She was crying profusely.
The erection was totally gone, my member dangling desolately.
"Get dressed. You're indecent, like this."
And he left.

CHAPTER NINE

The girl was very young, very beautiful. Ethereal.

He wanted to brush against me, but how could he, my arms were gone.

A strange itch had taken their place.

It floated. You didn't need legs. But arms! Even if it was only to brush the hair back from my face or to revive it. Would it last? Would they grow back? I was not familiar with this new form. I knew I could manifest and move objects. The play of the pictures had been very apt. He had remained soft. I giggled, still a woman of humor. How could I touch myself? Actually, they had made me very envious. They were copulating like rabbits in heat, and me? Without my arms, I couldn't even afford a caress!

The young woman had fallen in love, she was on her first experience, he could tell by the way she kissed him. Now she was getting dressed, she had rinsed her face, maybe she wanted to leave.

I thought about moving a chair. Maybe a chair was too conspicuous, she would start screaming like an eagle again.

Then a brush. The one from the toilet.

It was mother-of-pearl, as chic as every detail in that shrine to death.

They had been good at cleaning his shroud, now the smell was definitely different.

I moved the brush a few inches. I did it!

I moved it to the edge of the toilet, it was very close, there was the thud. She turned around. She was distracted, what was she thinking?

She picked up the brush. I could show myself in the mirror again, slowly, without frightening her. Certainly armless, white as a corpse, naked and with the gash in her chest... it was hard not to look creepy.
The lights went out. Suddenly. The girl let out a little sob, like a wail. Now she was frightened. The door opened. I didn't want to look, yet my eyes were glued. I had to know.
He came in. He was as tall and strong as she remembered. With those big, muscular shoulders. He was completely naked. With an erect cock. The creep, he was a sadist.
Naked except for the usual stocking over his head.
The girl stepped back and tapped on a pillar of the four-poster bed. This time I saw no knives.
I was surprised, I imagined it would take longer, after dinner at least. There was a certain savoir faire to dying after a good meal and with an earned orgasm. The poor thing would die a virgin and fasting.
He jumped on her, he had a full syringe, he stuck it in her neck and injected. The girl fell into a fitful sleep.
He shouldered her, she was a helpless body.
Inescapable end. But he wanted to see where it led.
He went down the stairs, it was still dark, he obviously knew the house well.
I followed him.
Little darling, she tossed her head from her long hair to the left and right, a few strands touching the filthy man's legs.
Maybe I could help her?

Maybe.

In truth it was more substantial for her now to discover the truth.

We all die.

It was a righteous revenge on the youth.

The one I lost.

He opened a room, the light here was blinding.

It was a lab.

As a doctor or surgeon.

He propped the girl up on an operating table.

He bound her torso and head with operating room ligatures.

Then he took four tourniquets and wrapped them, two, at the level of the biceps and, two, at the level of the thighs.

He'd cut her.

He put a mask over her mouth. It was certainly a sleeping pill. Perhaps he had the decency not to operate on her while she was conscious.

He washed his hands at a sink with disinfectant solution. He wore surgical gloves.

He cut off her clothes and got rid of them. Everything except her shoes.

She was naked.

He took a surgical cutter and began to cut the first arm. When he made the cut he was completely covered in blood.

He sutured the tissues and healed them. The blood stopped gushing.

The limb lay on the ground. The girl was biting her nails and on her thumb was a bit of residual pink nail polish.

He switched to his leg. He was out of breath, his chest rising and falling. The creep always had an erect dick.

The leg fell to the ground.

That's a nice, firm thump. Nice white tennis. Teenager.

He sutured, healed. He was methodical. He didn't want to kill her. Just amputate her limbs. And then what?

Because she was dead?

Now the other two limbs, hours had passed. The practice was interspersed with mouthfuls of sleeping pills. He had been a gentleman, perhaps not wishing for the little girl's screams.

She was done.

He attached a solution of painkiller and physiological saline to the young girl's stump and lastly he cut her hair. A nice cut indeed, short, comfortable, with jaunty bangs. He wiped the blood splatter off her face.

He cleaned the rest of the body. Unfortunately he had made a real mess, blood was everywhere, impregnating the small room with its iron smell.

Large patches were already clotting on the ground. I had never seen animals being slaughtered, but I supposed it was similar. Maybe no narcotic was used.

The girl was lying still on the cot. Naked without her limbs.

He unlocked the cot. He headed for another door. My attention reddened.

He walked up to a door, I hadn't noticed it before. It was a door with locks for cold storage. Defiladed behind carts of surgical implements displayed in order on a bed of sterilized cloths.

He opened it.

In truth, it was not cold. I went in with him. There was a small light bulb hanging. and many cots arranged concentrically.

On each cot were laid and meticulously bound the living busts of many women.

They were nude. They had beautiful faces, pale, terrified, with pronounced cheekbones, vivid lipsticks on their lips, eye shadows and mascara on their eyes, fashionable eyeliner, simple hairstyles, sometimes even their hair pulled back in vexatious tails. They were alive. They had no arms, no legs.

They were all naked, lying on the beds.

He counted them quickly, maybe thirty, maybe more. An acidic gag went up her throat. The dead, do they vomit?

He made room. He caressed them, whispered sweet words to them, called them by name. He moved two of them. It was neat.

You'll take off your sock, damn you.

Because not her. Because she was dead?

He returned to Clara's cot.

She was still narcotized.

He pushed it in.

He introduced her.

I still felt an excess of bile rise in my throat.

He put the cot in the middle of the amputee circle.

He took hold of his cock and penetrated Clara.

I vomited all over myself. The vomit came out in one violent gag and spread over my breasts and wound.

Hot. Oddly enough. I wasn't dead?

He enjoyed it immediately, the filthy, screamed sinking his cock violently into her inexperienced sex. He ejaculated, clearly satisfied.

I looked around. Some of the women were pregnant.

That's all I could see.

He left.

She was sad, desolate. Even I, who had seen and experienced much ugliness, could not imagine such barbaric human filth.

CHAPTER TEN

Helena fastened her boot laces. Her muscles darted happily. Athletic and limber, she admitted no argument. She was tough. A wrestler.
Many people assumed that wrestling was a sport for actors, instead it was a tough, almost acrobatic discipline of wrestling. To prepare herself she had undergone extremely hard training in boxing and falls, sumo and American wrestling. She had lived two years with an equestrian circus, had jumped from the quadrilateral to catch the trapeze and several times had fallen into the rescue net without breath. But she had always gotten back up. And now at the age of thirty-two she was British Women's Wrestling Champion. Unfortunately wrestling didn't have the followers it once had, it had gone from a stadium of 40,000 people to 400 screaming spectators. She was satisfied anyway. Her character was Wira, the Viking. She wore a gold stage costume with a long cloak and an axe as a weapon which she naturally left to the referee before entering the ring. She was loyal, they had never found anything on her during the search before the fight start. And she had always kept to the bargain, if she had to lose in order to grow her character's notoriety, she did so artfully and always without overdoing it. Wira, was a beloved character in wrestling circles.
And that's how she had to support herself.
She got on her motorcycle. She loved Italian bikes, her was a beautiful Ducati 916 sps. Red of course, single-seater. With a tapered tail with a

red central band and white side panels and the ever-present Superbike and World Champion sticker.
It was a rare piece, shee had bought it in Milan, years ago, with very few kilometres, completely original, still with the mark of the little Cagiva elephant, from the factory that later burned down, which moved production to Bologna, making the famous Borgo Panigale company famous. Unfortunately, every now and then, especially when cleaning it, the light clusters would fog up, the cat's eyes, designed by Mr. Tamburini, the engineer who designed it. The only flaw, for the rest it not only had a sensual and modern line, despite being made in 1997, but it was still very fast with its four injectors pumping in the two valves. It was a desmodromic engine, not yet a redhead, but still a high performance and powerful engine, which kept up with many supersport machines.
She put on her helmet and lowered her visor. She was expected in London for lunch.
Once the engine was started, there was the famous squeaky sound of the timing belt, enhanced by the carbon Termignoni.
She gears up at first, and off she goes.
The road was full of beautiful curves, which was why she had chosen the bike to go to London. She knew that road very well and it was exhilarating for an agile and slender biker like her.
The only drawback was the rain. She had in fact chosen the right tyres, the Pirelli Diablo Rosso Corsa were suitable for the cold and sometimes slippery asphalt.

The street was deserted, yet it was summer. And it was still raining, she would never get used to the London weather.
She heard a round, roaring noise reach her, another motorcycle for sure.
She saw it in the mirror, a naked car.
It was getting closer.
She let it get closer, she had a desire for a motorcycle duel, it would break the monotony of a deserted road.
There he is.
It was a boy on a silly black Triumph.
She wore goggles that were supposed to cover her and protect her from air and insects, with her helmet open and a handkerchief over her mouth. But what could a handkerchief protect?
She only chose full face helmets and full body suits with back protectors. It's no wonder she was so fast. Because she felt confident and unbeatable.
Come on, come on with your half-bike...
He shifted into fifth and accelerated. Lost him immediately. At the first corner, he downshifted, waited for her. There she was, she wasn't letting up, she'd accelerated as well. The bike must have been the latest generation, because it seemed to have excellent torque and good horsepower.
That would have been fun.
They continued for a few curves chasing each other, the road was really deserted. On a straight stretch she pulled away from him. But

the rain made her slow down. Now it was getting heavier. She climbed, better not to risk it. He passed her.

Patience. The safety of your bike, first and foremost.

She curved again then noticed a rivulet of smoke rising from the road.

The biker was down.

The bike was smoking a few miles away, laid out as well.

Deficient, he had evidently slipped.

She stopped.

She dismounted and approached the biker.

He was prone.

She touched his shoulder.

"Help me get your helmet off, I'm a doctor."

"Yes right away."

She opened her visor, with the rain he could already see nothing.

She turned it over. She really shouldn't have, you don't move a body. But if he was a doctor...

She unbuckled her helmet and lowered her scarf.

"Please remove my glasses and helmet. I'm fine don't worry. I was protected."

Helena nodded in the affirmative. He proceeded.

"Better, thank you. I'm breathing now."

"Help me up please."

"I don't think I can, she must weigh at least 90 kilograms. I only weigh 60 kilograms."

She had learned all her life to never expose herself first. That's how you win in the ring. Flying like pigeons and attacking like eagles.
She held a stick out to him and he rose.
He was as tall as she imagined, maybe even six feet, well placed, broad shoulders, red beard.
A handsome man.
"I'm fine."
"Can you take me home? I'm not far away. I live in Brungenwald."
"But you're leaving the Triumph here?"
"If you help me, I'll get it off the street. Then my mechanic will take it."
"Okay."
We lifted the bike with difficulty, it weighed about 190 kg, and pushed it to the edge of the road.
"Can you carry me? It looks like a single-seater."
"In fact no, I couldn't, the frame is flimsy, you'd be leaning on the exhausts heating them up too much. I can go into town and get some help for you though."
"My shoulder hurts. It's not true that I'm not hurt. I'll reimburse you for any damage."
"The damage to my bike is non-refundable. Besides, I didn't tell you to speed up like a daredevil."
"Help me, please, I want to lie down and take a painkiller. I'm going to get an x-ray in the morning."

"okay you can sit on the outside edge of the seat. As luck would have it, I'm tiny and don't take it all up. I'll push myself up on the tank, we should fit. For the lack of pedals, you'll have to make do, but please don't stand with your legs dangling, I don't have a scooter. ”

"I could lean my boots against the trellis."

"I see no other way. Know that I'm sorry, I'm only doing this out of solidarity."

"Okay thanks then, you're a good girl."

"Get in, come on, put your helmet on."

They both climbed in, miraculously it worked.

She went slowly, She didn't go over 40mph.

Brungenwald was close by, 20 km or so. She could already see the first settlements at the fourth bend.

She shouted to be heard over the Termignoni, "Where shall I take you?"

"At the house down the street, you see it, it has the crests of my household and is surrounded by roses."

It was true, here it is. Nice Victorian house, typically English.

She stopped the bike in front of the wooden door.

"Here we are, the taxi service has arrived at its destination."

He came down.

She didn't turn the bike off. I wanted to keep going.

"Can you please come down? I need your insurance information."

"How? Even? No come on... I have to move on, I'm not interested in your compensation. You're rich, it's obvious. Buy the bike back, it's probably ruined."
"Exactly, please be cooperative, if you state that we were close and I went off the road inside the speed limit and because of the wet asphalt, the insurance company will probably compensate me for the damage. I just need your details, then my secretary will contact you. Five minutes."
"Of course you're persistent. It's okay for the bike to rest. Do you have anywhere to keep it dry? Otherwise I won't stop if it stays in the rain."
"But yes of course, I have the garage. Dry and warm. Also for resting tires and engine."
"All right then."
"I'll show you, follow me."
She got on the bike again, lowered the visor, now she couldn't see anything.
The rain was pouring down. My goodness, it was summer!
The garage was just a few meters away, he opened the doors and motioned me to park in the motorcycle spot. Together with the bike there were two Bentleys and a Porsche 996 really very charming, white with blue stripes.
"You can leave your helmet on the bike."
She took off her helmet.

Her features were as firm as her personality. Knowing that males liked her. Black eyes, thick black eyebrows, and honey hair pulled back into a long braid. She was the Viking.

In wrestling if you're beautiful, you get the best characters.

"Come, perhaps some hot tea, it will soothe you. Or some hot broth. My housekeeper cooks a capon broth, wonderful."

"Broth is fine, thank you."

She followed him into the house.

He led her to a study.

"Do you want to take off your suit?"

"Yeah alright, underneath I've got my sock knit and t-shirt. Okay."

"Where?"

"Wherever you want. I have five guest rooms and five bathrooms."

"If you give me a room, this is where it gets long. Point me to the service bathroom or I'll take it off here in the study and it'll be quicker."

She was used to undressing in front of men, in wrestling the matches were often promiscuous and the locker rooms unique due to lack of funds.

She unzipped her jacket and started to take it off.

She seemed uninterested; he was rummaging through the drawers of a mahogany desk.

She took off her boots and took off her suit. Then she put the boots back on. And underneath she was wearing a tight-fitting Kevlar suit. Very comfortable.

"You're muscular."

"Like many."

"Broth"? And then the statement. So I'll change too, I'm all wet."

"Yeah okay."

"I leave you in the capable hands of Mrs. Boff. I'll go upstairs and put on a suit and be with you."

An elderly Lady appeared, plump, walking badly, perhaps her knee ligament was torn or healed, however sore.

"You caught a cold out there."

"It's summer, unbelievable moorland."

"Come into the kitchen. I'll serve you something hot. You'll be fine afterwards."

The kitchen was huge, with a gaudy window to the garden.

The light came in copiously, reflecting off the hanging steel pans. A beautiful white table and two benches stood in the middle. I sat down.

"Here, drink up."

The smell was fantastic, of meat cooked for hours on low heat to capture the fat and cartilage. It was packed with protein.

I drank, feeling the warm liquid run down my throat, to my stomach.

I was a little tired, actually. My head was spinning. Maybe I had overdone even jogging this morning for all those miles, almost 20 miles, even if it was flat, it was quite an effort. My head was spinning.

"Excuse me, can I have some water?"

Her mouth was swollen, She was seeing double, She looked drunk.

But she was fine before. What was in the soup? WHAT DID YOU PUT IN MY SOUP? She got up, she couldn't talk, everything was spinning, everything was spinning.

And then it was dark.

CHAPTER ELEVEN

I watched as the blonde fell to the ground.

It made quite a bang.

She was less bony than the last three.

In fact she looked muscular and toned.

By now I had fallen into a kind of apathy. I no longer frequented the room of horrors. He'd try to scare them, some of them would smell fear and try to escape. But he always took them back. Now he'd started drugging them. It eliminated the problem of escape.

I imagined he wanted to get rid of me, regretted killing me.

When I knew where my body was, then I would be gone for good. I was disgusted. Better to end up in hell.

There he was, he had heard the thud.

He took her in his arms. This time like a woman, not like a sack of meat ready for slaughter.

He wasn't naked, but he had a stocking over his head. Mrs. Boff had disappeared. He was wearing a light cotton suit and a T-shirt.

He led her to the first floor, opened the lavender room, the one with the canopy bed. He put her down on the bed, in the middle.

From the pockets of the suit, he took more socks and began to tie them to the edges of the bed. Hands and feet. This one was different. It had stimulated his imagination.

He took the scissors and cut through the Kevlar. He released her, leaving her bra and panties on.

She was actually very muscular. She was lean and toned but with all the muscles well defined.

She was definitely a sportswoman.

She groaned, waking up.

"Where am I? What happened? WHY AM I TIED UP!"

"You needn't fear, we'll have fun, then I'll let you go."

"I HATE MEN! LEAVE ME NOW!"

A lesbian. This is where the fun begins.

She looked astonished, stood still for a second. She had never heard that voice before from the sock man. I had never heard that voice before. It sounded like a puerile little voice. Different.

This was a tough one, she had intimidated him, perhaps.

He also looked vaguely inky, less robust than usual, perhaps shorter.

I decided to help the girl, I untied a stocking, only partially, she would do the rest. One of the left ankle. She noticed the play she was allowed on the left.

"Come closer, I can't hear. What do you want from me?" He came closer.

Then I saw her draw air into her lungs, tighten her abdominals and deliver a powerful straight-leg kick aimed at his head.

She hit him, the surprise and force injected benefited her, he lost his balance and hit the other edge of the bed, completely off balance.

I decided to unbuckle the other foot as well. Here I would finally have some fun.

Then the blonde girl curled up into an egg and kicked with her feet together directly into his face. It hit him fully and flew off the bed onto the floor. A large trickle of blood stained the stocking at nose level. 'At last we see your blood, you swine.

She crouched down again into an egg and reached for the stocking that bound her left arm. She introduced her foot and pulled so far, spreading the stocking, that she could free her hand. She had risen again.

He stared at her from the edge of the bed, standing there completely dumbfounded.

Stupid human being. Did you think you were invincible?

She snatched at the canopy pole nailing the last wrist with both hands, levered up her legs, and delivered another kick, aimed at his stomach. I could clearly feel the air and saliva coming from his mouth. It was too easy...

She crouched down to catch her breath, she understood now, that her opponent was better than the others.

She released her other hand. She may have injured her left wrist, but she didn't stop. She quickly stood upright, moving away from the soft mattress, and searching the hard floor.

She clenched her fists. And she started to jump. She was a boxer. It was great!

She approached him with her feet apart, hopping but you could tell she was planted on the ground. She let loose a left jab and a right jab, jaw and cheekbone at him, who lost his balance and staggered back.

Then he approached, protecting his face with his fists and leaning over, an uppercut directed at his stomach.

He stooped to the ground, crouching.

Then she did something I'd only seen at wrestling matches, leapt upward, pirouetted to crash with her elbow outstretched, into his stomach on the ground. She started coughing.

She held him to the ground. She jumped up again to landslide with both feet outstretched to hit him with her heels and the full weight of her body.

He chose the pubes.

She had knocked him out.

She could hear him whimpering like a little girl. He was holding his belly and his dick. It was a disgusting sight.

He was to warn this goddess of the others, that he would free them, or kill them, or both. And that he would discover her body.

We heard footsteps.

It could have been Mrs. Boff.

She hid behind the door. She was so smart.

The door was thrown open. It was Henry, red beard, blue eye. There was no doubt about it.

I was shocked. I had always assumed it was him, but it wasn't.

"What are you doing, you idiot! Get up! Where's the girl? I told you it was a long shot, I could tell she was tough."

Who the man on the ground was. They knew each other.

"Take off your sock fool, you can't understand what you're saying and then you don't breathe. You broke your teeth! You're bleeding!"
"It's wi, it's WI I was in orta!"
"What are you saying moron, take off this sock, he gave them to you like you were a beardless kid!"
Henry bent over him, and released him from the stocking.
It was the mechanic! The mechanic who had taken her car, the Smart car to be fixed!"
The anger that mounted in me was irremediable.
Filthy scum, you were accomplices!
I always wondered why the police never looked for me.
The mechanic pointed behind Henry.
There was the fighter, she was ready. She spun around on her outstretched leg and hit Henry in the neck. He went over the side.
Then she took his head between her thighs and tipped him over, using his weight. The thud on the floor was like a side of beef on the butcher's counter.
Henry was on the ground, supine.
She leaned to the side and still planted her elbow directly into his stomach.
Then she got back up and kicked him side-footed, on his exposed hip. He was a real sack. She took his head and pounded it hard on the wooden foot of the four-poster bed. A sound of bruised wood echoed in the silence.
She had the advantage, she could run.

Come on, go.

She saw the phone, picked it up and dialed the local police number, 111.

"I'm at Mr. Henry's house, it's on fire, quickly come in force, a fire is spreading."

This was truly the progenitor of a superior race.

She went downstairs.

Sirens could be heard, in the distance, it was all over.

They would have found out everything.

The women, the murders, the brutality, the abuse.

There's the squad car. It was parking. The policeman got out,

"Miss, we received an urgent call, reporting a fire, but I don't see any flames, and there you are in your underwear. Where's the Count?"

"I'll explain everything. I'm in my underwear because they drugged me and wanted to rape me and then who knows what."

"Where are they? Were there more than one of them?"

"Yeah in two, I beat them up good. They're knocked out. This Henry and another one, never seen him. Upstairs."

"The policeman signaled to his companion to come down."

They were strong, trained, tall. She had a terrible déjà vu. Tears came up, She recognized him.

He killed her.

"Miss, come closer, we'll protect you now."

NOOOOO

I HAVE TO WARN YOU!!! DON'T GO!!! IT'S THEM!!! THEY. ALL THEM!!!!!
I started the car siren.
She paused. She was on alert again.
I moved the car forward to put it between them and her.
"What's going on? Did you take the keys out?"
"No, I mean yes, I put the handbrake on. I don't know how it moved."
"Miss, come on, we'll take you to the station."
I started the sirens again.
"What's going on? Get in the car, check it out!"
Why did you kill me? You didn't even rape me, just killed me. For the blood? For the adrenaline? Because you felt like the alpha male? I wasn't strong enough yet, but I wanted to throw the car at him, right over his head, and see him crushed miserably under its weight of sheet metal.
The girl was getting closer, they were going to grab her and take her back to the house.
"Come on, be a good girl, we'll get you to sign the statement, we need to take you to the station, get in the car..."
Perhaps it was the Sergeant's insistence, or the fact that he kept one hand resting on the baton tucked into his belt and one forward to grab her arm as soon as she came within range, that alerted the boxer.
I saw her retreat. Back up the steps and up the porch. She was considering how to move, what her chances were.
The bike was in the garage.

The garage was 100 yards away on the right, beside the porch.
Behind her she had two individuals pinned down but would recover within a few minutes, maybe a dozen.
She had the two cops in front of her. The first one weighed 180 pounds and the second one, about 95. The second one was aggressive and well planted. The other one was hesitating, he was obviously subservient to the first one.
She didn't have her motorcycle boots on, she was barefoot, impossible to ride like that. They were in the study on the ground floor.
Helmet was on the bike. Ditto the keys to start it in the ignition box.
She had gas for at least 60 miles, she'd get to the next town.
She decided on a motorcycle getaway. She was going to wrap her toes for change with rags for tightness. Or with her bra and panties, if she hadn't found them in the garage. The garage had a door of the old non-electric kind, she remembered it perfectly, she had jerked open the two wooden doors.
Step one, lay down the aggressive, as fast as you can.
The other would have been stunned.
She was smart, sensing the adrenaline coursing through her veins fast, she positioned herself on her killer's right side, the baton side. She brought her fists up to protect her ribcage, neck and face. She was small, barely reaching the other man's torso.
She set off her right arm, grabbed his and twisted it, using all her weight to twist and break it.

He was stunned. He heard a sharp snap of bones, began to yell, "BITCH."

He tried to grab her hair with his left, the one still healthy, the other dangling like a limp dick from her arm. She dodged and set off a straight leg kick, spinning around to gain power. The kick caught him in the neck. She staggered.

She had an advantage.

The other one was moving, She advanced the car until she hit him in the legs, lightly but the surprise, made him fall to his knees. Run baby, run. You've got the advantage, keep it. The other two could have been here any minute.

The girl ran to the garage. It was locked.

Damn it. Bolt.

Something to break it.

Anything to break it? Now!

I moved the gardener's spade, I literally moved it, it flew over the heads of those present, as in comic strips of little imagination, and stopped beside her.

She turned her head left and right. "There's no one there dear, I'm here, evanescent and impalpable, a spirit, a dead woman with no arms or legs, covered in my own vomit, with a gash in my chest that looks like the New York Turnpike.

Now open the latch like a good girl. You'll think about what you didn't understand about the facts later".

She slipped the spade perpendicular to the latch and pulled at herself, unhinged the lock, and threw open the door.
"YOU BITCH, YOU BROKE MY ARM!"
They were coming. There's the bike.
Keys. Perfect.
There were no rags. What was She doing? Stripping?
She wrapped her bra to the tip of her left foot and her panties to her right foot. She mounted the bike, turned on the ignition. Engaged first gear. It thundered through the closed walls of the garage. “This is a great bike. Too bad I didn't learn it in life.”
Back. Helmet on, not lowered, visor up. Why didn't she fasten it?
Now she had the boss in front of her, carousing towards her, holding her dangling arm.
He revved the bike, the wheel screeching on the gravel, the brake applied. The nose pointed at the attacker.
She wanted to charge him, like a bull in the arena.
She let off the brake, the bike reared up and headed straight for him.
She grabbed the helmet with her right hand, extended her arm and charged it with the full power of his bike's speed into the attacker's chest.
He flew to the ground. She braked, drifted with the rear, skidding 180 degrees, coming back again with her muzzle on her attacker on the ground, breathless.
She let go of the brake and literally rode on top of him with all 200 kg of his red Ducati.

Then she braked again, returned to first gear, turned the bike more slowly and headed for the exit. She put her helmet on properly, lowered the visor and fastened it.

“Thank you, intense.”

On the patio Henry and the mechanic had come down.

They helped the third one to his feet.

She'd won, she could go. What was keeping her?

They had the car.

She was naked with temporary shoes, she couldn't handle a chase.

She returned to the garage, there were other cars.

She raised her visor.

Gasoline, acids, motor oil, some thumb wrenches, a screwdriver, some motorcycle stands.

She started the Bentley. They were coming, she could hear them. And the Porsche.

She opened the hood of the Porsche. Old engines, poor safety.

She dumped all the gasoline on it. It was dripping all the way to the manifolds.

That's great.

She got back on the bike.

She could now turn back towards the trio.

She found them side by side proceeding compactly with batons in their hands.

They were halfway between the police car parked at the entrance and the garage that would soon detonate.

They wanted to throw her off the bike, she didn't have enough room to gain acceleration.
“She needed me.”
She blatantly turned the throttle of the bike and lowered her visor.
He wanted to be the cue ball.
He was afraid for her.
He took off, it was the game of the tough guys, whoever gave in got unhorsed.
It pointed straight at Henry, in the middle.
He ducked at the last, claw at her chest, and pulled her off the bike.
The ducati wandered for two minutes then planted itself on the car.
Helena was on the ground, her helmet had protected her head, but her body was excoriated in her back and buttocks.
She was bleeding.
He stood up with a small leap.
Henry wanted to catch her, I opened the front door, she needed to take cover, find some weapons, some shoes. And fight.
She understood, ran to the door and closed it behind him. She was too agile, Henry missed her by a second and found the door slammed against her. I held it shut with her.
I could feel them.
"OPEN UP BITCH!!!"
It was time to show her their little play, she would understand and imagine a suitable remedy.
She was bleeding.

She took off her helmet.

In the study she found the boots, put them on at once. The overalls were useless, they would clog every movement.

I opened another door for her, sideways in the hallway.

"Who's here?"

“Did you understand? We didn't have time for bold and beautiful Helena.”

“Go ahead, ask the questions later.”

She lit the stairwell light for her.

It was obvious, She had to get off.

Don't worry, I'll close every window and every door for you.

They won't come in yet.

Helena, went down the steps, one at a time, she was hesitant.

Another door, wide open for her, another corridor lit up.

“Be a good girl, follow the breadcrumbs, they will lead you to the horrible truth.”

“You saw the operating room, it was spotless. Mrs. Boff was a wonderful housekeeper.”

She was sorry to upset her, she was such a good girl.

She opened the last door.

The spectacle was gruesome.

The hospital beds, methodically arranged in a circle.

Thirty-four women, three in advanced stages of pregnancy.

Armless, legless, with scarred stumps, tied at the waist and throat to their coffins.

Made up and combed, some shaved in the genitals, completely naked. Two of them had silver piercings embellishing their nipples.

Lots of pain relief and saline solutions hanging from the cots. Sedatives for pain and agony.

They were alive, awake. Pissed off.

"Who are you? How did you get here?"

"Are you with the police?"

"You're naked! He wanted to cut you...you ran away! Where is he?"

"Did you kill him?"

"Call the police!"

"No! Kill me! I can't take another minute of this life."

"Kill me too."

Clara spoke, beautiful Clara, her blonde hair had grown a little, now cut short.

"I think I'm pregnant, I haven't had my period in two months, I think it's two months, time seems relative. Please kill me. I can't go back to my parents, my friends."

She was sobbing.

Helena was wiping away her tears, I hadn't noticed her crying. She cried like men do, silently, long tears dripping from her eyes, onto her chest and onto the ground.

She whispered, "I can't. Please, I'll call a doctor. They'll fit you with prosthetics. I'm sure there's a way to fix it."

"He raped me every day! He comes in with a hard cock and shoves it down my throat! You can't fix that!"

"Me too, they move the cots to the centre, I think they are different, even if they wear stockings, one time one is fat, the other is shorter. Then there is the doctor. He has a beard, you can see it under the stocking."

"I know them by their dicks. They're all different."

"They also do it with the dildo, in the ass, they put us in the middle. For the others. Then they turn us as they want, we are stumps anyway. LET ME DIE!"

"No me, I can't do it. I have to go now, they're outside. I have to get to the real police and get a doctor here."

Helena, you couldn't understand. There was no way to fix it.

This was an inescapable present.

She wiped her tears with her arm.

I slammed the door twice.

She understood on the fly, turned and ran down the stairs, we could hear their screams in the distance.

I led her to the kitchen.

Turn on the stove.

"Who's here with me?" She had a small voice now, she was really scared. I didn't want to take away her strength, I wanted to help her.

Mrs. Boff appeared in the doorway.

"What's going on? Who's knocking on the door like that?"

Fat old woman, you knew everything and you tolerated it. You cooked your stupid meat soup and thought that with a swollen belly, we'd be raped more happily.

At that moment a thunderous roar moved the air.

"What's going on? Sweet Jesus! It's an explosion!"

Helena gave her a compact punch to the belly and a well-aimed one to the jaw. We distinctly heard a crick. She was probably broken now.

The old woman fell on the cold marble of the kitchen.

I raised the flame of the fires.

"Who are you?" Helena looked up at the ceiling.

Silly, I'm right behind you.

But we don't have time for conversation, and besides, I've always been a woman of facts.

I blew on the flame of the fires.

The smell of gas was overwhelming now.

Helena coughed.

I opened the window to the garden. What beautiful willows, how well they moved in the warm wind from the fire that burned in the garden. Soon it would reach the house.

Henry and his fellow raiders had headed to the garage, were trying to put out the flames with two fire hydrants.

We could bet, would the firemen arrive first or the fire at the mansion? And how long would it take for it to explode?

Helena took the long way around, returned to the entrance, picked up the bike.

It was rifled in the nice red fairings, but still running.

She was no longer wearing a helmet, but now she was wearing boots.

"I'm leaving, thank you. Can you hear me? Thank you."

He turned on the gas and was gone in minutes.

I looked at her, I liked Helena.

CHAPTER TWELVE

Helena stopped at the Bistro from the bus stop.

She was naked, upset.

He had to at least make a phone call and borrow some clothes.

He entered, the door rang, alerting the person at the counter.

A tall, middle-aged, ruby-haired woman with a few strands of greasy hair stuck haphazardly to the top of her head came towards her.

"What happens at the count's house? You come from there! You're naked! You have escaped. We heard a terrible bang!"

There are the sirens. The house was detonated.

"I need to make a phone call. And I need some clothes."

"DID I ASK YOU WHAT HAPPENED TO COUNT HENRY?"

Helena warned herself. She was too aggressive, why that reaction?

"I don't know. I fell on my bike."

He backed slowly toward the door.

"YOU KNOW! YOU'RE NAKED! YOU REBELLED! YOU ESCAPED."

"Escaped from what?"

"You want to rebel, you want to be an emancipated woman, with a motorbike, your tits in the wind...we have a lot of fun here with people like you, you know!?"

"Yeah, you guys really play nice."

The woman had turned red, a vein throbbing relentlessly at the level of her temple.

She stopped in the middle of the room. Her legs were spread apart and she was breathing heavily, trying to inhale all the air in the room through his nose and mouth.

Her eyes seemed to pop out of her orbital socket so wide they were.

Helena had gained the front door, pushed with one hand lightly to get out. The trill.

A swollen, soft belly stopped her.

"Where are you going pretty pussy?"

An ordinary man in a red and white plaid shirt, rolled up sleeves and faded jeans. He smelled like dung. He had a horrible Harlequin mustache.

"I like my dinners...don't go away just yet."

He was holding a sharp cleaver, the kind used to slice meat.

She slid it all the way into Helena's abdomen, horizontally like a beautiful, classy belt.

Helena was stunned. Had it really happened?

After all that effort, she'd gotten skewered by a putrid belly that resembled a Hells Angels?

"You don't want me to go on a diet right now when meat tastes this good?"

They took her.

She was dying. She could feel her heartbeat racing and the blood draining. She had to calm down or it would have helped the blood flow. Maybe it was her liver.

She had read that it was a very painful death. She felt nothing now.

An idea. An idea that would earn her salvation.

She staggered toward the center of the pub. Her vision blurred.

The woman stepped back. She didn't want to get dirty?

Blood was pouring out, dripping down his legs, dripping onto the ground.

"Help." It was faint. With an immovable point. Life was slipping away between her legs. And she was dying naked in boots, with a cleaver stuck in her belly cutting her in two.

The woman sneered.

Helena fell to her knees.

She tried with her hands to dab at the wound.

Oh, my God, there was so much blood. It was dark red, thick. Venous. She was a goner.

"We'll cook this one, it's muscular, the meat will have to be marinated well, otherwise it stays stringy."

They ate them. They ate the arms and the legs and of some, the whole body.

They would have eaten her.

The disgust was overwhelming, the nausea was overwhelming, causing her to regurgitate adrenaline.

NOOOOOOO

She charged like a bull at the woman's head.

I DON'T WANT TO DIE.

Was he screaming it? Yet in his head it was a powerful scream.

The bitch fell on the floor.

The Hells Angels approached, hands forward like the living dead, mumbled something like *I'll catch you*. But she couldn't hear them now. The thunders of her heart thundered in her head. She had little time before she passed out and bled to death. She wasn't going to die alone. She was never going to get flab in that stinking man's filthy belly.

She entered the kitchen. He chased her, but he was clumsy.

He had lost track of the old woman.

In the back she saw a door.

She pushed it with his shoulder. She held her cleaver and her belly. She took a cloth and wrapped it to compact that new sculpture into her abdomen. It had to keep the blood from draining quickly.

More cars parked outside. A red Chevy had its window down, it was open. She got in. She rolls up the window and locks the car. The asshole slams his fat ass down on the closed door. He's railing and pounding on the hood with his stubby hands.

There were no keys.

Easy, Helena, easy. Fuck! What calm? I'm bleeding to death!

She took the cables under the steering wheel, cut them and pulled them closer. The car started.

It was an automatic transmission.

Nobody wanted to drive in gears anymore.

She put the car in reverse, the big man stepped back, not expecting it. She stepped back again, then accelerated and struck him full in the waist.

He bounced off the hood.

Helena put the back up.

He baked like a loaf of bread taken out of the oven, on the asphalt.

She pushed the accelerator into drive and passed over him once.

Then she put it in reverse, and passed it back.

She saw the crushed head on the asphalt.

She had to decide, did she die there in that car?

Trying to get into a hospital in London?

She had a range of 250 km. She could have made it.

And the wound, it would hold for about an hour.

No. Definitely not.

But hope, that subtle hook with survival, drove her to London.

She turned the car around.

And she left quickly.

EPILOGUE

The police found the red Chevrolet a few miles from London, the driver, recognized as Helena Dickinson, had died from an obvious blunt weapon attack.

The autopsy revealed no altered states.

No connection to the owner of the car, picked up in the town of Buchenwald a few miles away, James Fricktorn, accountant.

Fricktorn states, "I had parked my car to have a snack at Angus's Bistro."

INDEX

UNA VITA DI STELLE LIBRARY
A.V. Italia S.r.l. Group
VAT number 03624001206

PUBLISHED AUGUST 14, 2021, BOLOGNA

Tacit assonances

Tacit assonances

www.ingramcontent.com/pod-product-compliance
Ingram Content Group UK Ltd.
Pitfield, Milton Keynes, MK11 3LW, UK
UKHW022018190726
13853UKWH00005B/2000

9 791280 619488